BLACK FRIDAY

by Dane G. Kroll

Books by Dane G. Kroll

Realm of Goryo: Prelude- Japan vs Mankind
Realm of Goryo: The Four Pillars
Realm of Goryo: The Culling
Realm of Goryo: The Riven Mother

Fantasy
Eluan Falls: The Inheritors of the World
Eluan Falls: The Tides of Utter Undoing

Horror
Psalm Springs
Black Friday

Dedicated to
Ashley
Finally, a friend
that likes horror movies

BLACK FRIDAY

Chapter 1

Every grueling second got the night closer to midnight. The bitter cold was only made worse by the invasive wind. Customers stood in line outside a giant building with four plain walls and a grand sign at the front entrance. There was no cover or shelter outside of the BestMart. The customer always came first, once they were inside the store.

It was the largest supermarket in the city. BestMart offered groceries, household items, clothing, electronics, toys, and much more. They were your one stop shop for anything and everything.

The line of people wrapped around two corners of the building. Each person was bundled up with several layers of sweaters, gloves, and stalking caps that tasseled inches into the air. The cold was not going to stop them from the deals of a lifetime.

BestMart's Black Friday sales were the best in the city. They would not only match any other store's offer, but they would also give a ten percent discount to the customer on their next shopping trip for choosing BestMart over their competitor.

The line continued to grow around the building as the clock ticked closer to midnight. The November chill was still settling in for the night. The back of the line was quiet. It was filled with frowns and words of disappointment. They should have been there hours ago if they wanted a better spot in line.

Many of the people in the front of the line had completely bypassed their Thanksgiving meals and time with their extended families for their prime spots in line. They sat in lawn chairs like kings on their thrones. Many of them even feasted on cold turkey legs to complete the look.

Peter Adams stood huddled next to his two sons, Jacob and Bobby. Peter tried to keep them as warm as he could. Bobby was more than happy to hug his dad's leg. Bobby was five. He was excited to stay up late with his dad on a mission to get his mom a wonderful Christmas gift. It was also the perfect time for Bobby to put his Christmas list together. He already knew the top of the list was going to be all five of the newest Battlebear toys.

Bobby watched every episode of the newest Battlebears show. It was the greatest cartoon ever, and Bobby could not get enough of it. Before, he had to dig through his older brother's former toys to find the previous incarnation of Battlebear toys. This year toys for the new show were coming out and Bobby wanted all of them. He was more than happy to go with his Dad shopping if it meant he could get a glimpse of the Battlebears.

Bobby's older brother, Jacob, was another story. He always kept at least three feet from his father and brother. He hadn't said a word since getting in the car to go to BestMart. His mom was out doing her own Black Friday shopping. Nobody was home and his parents were not going to let Jacob stay home alone for the night. He was fourteen, but despite his protests Jacob was going to have to go with his dad to help watch Bobby. So Jacob rolled his eyes and got in the van.

"When can we go in?" Bobby asked. "I'm cold."

"Just another ten minutes," said Peter. "You'll be okay."

"I'm tired," said Bobby.

"I know, but once we're inside there will be plenty to look at."

"Can I get a Battlebear?" Bobby asked. His faced beamed back to excitement.

"If you're good," said his dad. "First, we have to get your mom that new tablet she wants. So keep an eye out for that. Then we can hurry to the toys and see what they have."

Bobby smiled back at his dad. He nodded his head in the affirmative.

Behind the locked glass doors of the BestMart, Richard, the assistant manager, came into view. Richard was a heavyset man that always kept a fake smile on his face.

He read once that if you put on a fake smile it would eventually turn into real happiness. He dangled his keys at the anticipating crowd outside. Then Richard tapped his watch and smiled coyly. There was still eight minutes until he unlocked the doors.

The little joke did not go over well with the crowd in the front of the line. They had been waiting for hours; some since the early morning. The line forced itself forward. People began to press themselves up against the glass to get as close as they could to the inside.

The movement caused a jumpstart in the line. Within seconds the line began to vanish. It was becoming a mob of people forcing their way toward the entrance of the BestMart.

The rush of people knocked Peter forward toward the building. He reached out for Bobby, but he could not grab his son's hand.

"Jacob," Peter yelled out. "Get Bobby!"

Jacob did as his father told. He forcibly grabbed Bobby's hand. Bobby was nearly yanked off of his feet by his older brother's roughness.

"Ow!" said Bobby. "I'm telling mom."

Peter tried to push his way back toward his children, but the crowd would not budge. Nobody wanted to move and risk losing their spot to somebody behind them. Peter was stuck.

Richard continued to stand just beyond the door. He watched the time like a hawk. Every movement of his was exaggerated. He thought he was being funny. He wanted to entertain the crowd outside in the last few minutes before he opened the store for Black Friday.

"Richard, what are you doing?" asked his boss, the general manager of BestMart, Howard. He was younger than Richard, but Howard had been the general manager for six years. He worked for BestMart for twice that. It was his first and only job. If there was one thing he did not like, it was Richard.

"I'm just trying to have a little fun with the customers," said Richard. "They love it! It's boring out there, you know."

"You've got them riled up, now," said Howard. "There are still a few minutes before we're supposed to open."

"Yeah, now they'll be all excited to get in and buy things. It's a business strategy."

"I wanted to keep this as orderly as possible."

"It'll be fine, Howard" said Richard. "Have some fun for once."

Howard did not answer. He rubbed his temples to encourage the headache he was getting to go away. One of these days he was going to be able to transfer Richard. One of these days.

"You really need to chill," said Richard. "This'll

be great. I'll record them coming through the doors. We'll make a viral video."

"I don't want any problems, Richard. Unlock the doors in a minute, and keep everybody moving. Direct them to where certain items are. I just want this to go smoothly."

"Got it!" said Richard.

Howard walked off. He had more things to check up on before they officially opened, and time was running out.

Richard turned back to the doors. He dangled his keys once again. The crowd grew agitated at his antics. Many of them began to pound on the glass. They were eager to get through the sliding glass doors.

"Only thirty seconds!" Richard yelled for all to hear.

Outside, Peter was getting frustrated. He kept looking back toward his sons. He could see the top of Jacob's head. Bobby was out of sight. Peter wanted desperately for the doors to open. He wanted the crowd to move so he could get back to his family.

"Open the doors!" Peter yelled out. The crowd responded with cheers.

Richard approached the lock. He slipped the key in slowly. Every move was a theatric. The assistant manager's eyes were wide with fake excitement and he had a giant smile plastered on his face.

The door cracked open an inch.

It was all that the crowd needed. Dozens of hands slipped through the opening and forced the double doors wide open. The line of customers was now a mob.

They rushed inside, away from the bitter cold and toward the warm presence of amazing sales. Richard ducked out of the way. He huddled in the corner of the lobby. He made no attempt at controlling the unruly crowd.

Peter was pushed forward. He could not fight against the crowd rushing into the store. People pushed and forced their way closer to their prizes. Peter watched one man stumble to the ground. Nobody came to help him. He was stepped over and stepped on as the crowd continued to pour into the building.

Jacob held tightly onto Bobby's hand. They lost their father completely. He was lost somewhere in the crowd.

"Let's go to the toys," suggested Bobby. He pulled on Jacob's hand to urge them in the direction of the Toy Department.

Jacob pulled against his little brother's arm. Bobby nearly lost his footing. Jacob kept walking with the mob of people. He was nearly dragging his brother along with him.

"I want to go to the toys!" Bobby said.

Jacob looked back at this brother, but did not

acknowledge him.

Peter continued to fight against the crowd to get back to his sons. He could not see them anymore, but it didn't stop him from trying. The plan to get his wife the tablet was long gone. He didn't care about that anymore. He wanted to find his children, and nobody was helping.

"Move. I need to find my kids," said Peter to the unmovable mob.

Items and sales were starting to be discovered all around the store, and word was getting out where they were. The excitement pushed the crowd even harder. Nobody wanted to miss out on the best deals of the year.

Peter finally had enough. He stopped moving all together. He was going to hold his place until he found his sons.

That did not go over well with the rest of the customers. They did not stop for him. Peter was knocked back and shoved to the side. He stumbled, but held his footing. The crowd kept knocking him back farther and farther.

Eventually, Peter was knocked to the side. He fell into a stack of holiday themed crackers. The boxes tumbled all around him. He could hear the crunch of snack food crumble under his weight.

Peter looked up to be greeted by a cardboard cutout of Santa Claus. Jolly Saint Nick was accompanied with a word bubble that read: *Happy Holidays!*

Peter stayed where he was. Relentless shoppers were finally not shoving past him. The crowd was out of control. Everywhere people were fighting for products that would later be treasured gifts to loved ones.

A man and a woman were fighting over a pair of sixty percent off sunglasses.

"Give me that! I saw it first."

"Too bad, I have it!"

A new mob of people crowded around a pile of smart TVs. They were the cheapest in town. One man started to climb over others in front of him to get to the TVs, but his weight was too much and he tumbled forward instead. It did not stop the rest of the crowd from continuing their pillage of the smart TVs.

Howard stepped carefully through the mob. He hated Black Fridays. No matter how hard he tried he could never get them to go smoothly. He already had to break up two fights, and he saw several more starting to break out. It was madness.

He watched as one woman fought her way through the crowd toward the toy section.

"Where are the Battlebears? My daughter needs a green Battlebear."

Howard looked over to his right. Two women were fighting over who knows what at that point. The item was long gone by another customer. It did not stop the two women from pulling each other's hair and dragging one another to the floor.

Just off to the side of the fight a young man was recording the fight with his phone.

"This is so cool," he said.

Howard moved quickly to jump into the fray and put an end to it.

Jacob stood quietly at the edge of the Clothing Department. His grip squeezed on Bobby's hand. The crowd was rushing past them in a frenzy to get to the electronics.

"I want to go!" demanded Bobby. "This is boring."

Jacob did not say a word.

"Let's go to the toys! I want a new toy!"

Bobby tried to walk forward toward the rushing river of people in the aisle. Jacob would not let him go.

It was nonstop. People all over the place were yelling and screaming at each other. More fights began to break out. Howard was breaking up a new fight about the right to buy the last lounge chair. One customer claimed he had more money and should be the one to get it. The other did not agree.

"Sir, unfortunately this is a first come first serve basis," Howard said to the supposedly rich man. "This gentleman already had possession of the chair. It's his if he wants it."

"I'll give you double for it," said the man with the fat wallet.

Howard looked at the man with confusion.

"It's his chair," Howard said once again. "You can get a raincheck at the register. Please continue shopping. Thank you."

Howard turned away at that point. There was no further point in talking to the guy that would pay more than regular price for an item on Black Friday.

He began to survey the area one more time. There was still a lot to cover, and many issues to solve. He could see one of the newer and more trusted employee, Heather, ushering out more dollar bin movies. She barely got them out to the floor before onlookers mobbed her and her crew.

Over in the Sports and Recreation Department, Taylor was supposed to be offering assistance to the customers. He was nowhere to be found. Howard would have to have a word with him later.

Jennifer only looked busy in the Jewelry Department. She was laughing with a group of customers that were surrounding her. They were all young girls, and none of them were shopping. He would have to talk with Richard about her.

Howard looked at his watch. It had only been fifteen minutes. It was going to be a long night. He did another quick pan of the area. Customers were everywhere. They were mostly sticking to the aisles. The best deals were in the back of the store.

There were a couple of outliers in other departments. Some customers figured it was quicker to navigate through the maze of clothes racks or the aisles with less popular appliances to find shortcuts around the store.

While Howard was looking around he caught sight of Jacob and Bobby. Bobby was trying to wiggle his way out of Jacob's grip. The young man did not move. He stayed put and just watched the rest of the crowd go along their way as they looked for the best deals.

Howard started to make his way toward the two brothers. He thought it was suspicious for Bobby to be fighting so hard to get out of Jacob's grip. It could be nothing, or it could be a kidnapping. Howard had to be on the safe side. It was his responsibility to oversee the safety of all of his guests at BestMart.

Bobby pulled against his brother's arm. He tried to yank his hand free from Jacob's iron grip. All the good toys would be gone if Jacob didn't let him go soon.

A new wave of customers started to pour in. This group was standing around the second corner of the line. They were cold and they were eager to get to the deals that were left.

Bobby paid no attention to the new rush of people. He was too busy trying to break free from his older brother. The young boy started to walk as hard as he could away from Jacob. He was leaning forward as far as he could to gain leverage. Jacob let his arm get stretched out to allow Bobby the most distance possible.

"Let go of me!" Bobby yelled. "I want to go to the toys. Dad said I could get a Battlebear if I was good. I've been good. Let me go!"

The crowd in front of the two boys was nonstop. They continued to push their way farther and harder than the people in the beginning of the line.

Jacob looked down at his little brother who was trying desperately to pull his arm out of his socket and get to the Toy Department.

Then Jacob shoved Bobby forward.

The little boy tried to regain his balance against the force of the push, but he flailed about instead and fell forward. Bobby went straight into the mob of people rushing toward the back of the store.

His hand was the last thing to be seen before the current of the mighty mob carried Bobby away.

Peter weaved through the other customers. They became so focused on the items in their carts they no longer noticed Peter cutting through them. The worried father looked all around for his sons.

He went to the Toy Department first. He

hoped Bobby had convinced Jacob to take him there. But Peter had no luck.

Then Peter began to look through every aisle. His head turned back and forth looking for his family.

Eventually, he reached the front of the store. The crowd was dissipating near the Clothing Department. On the ground was what looked like a heap of clothing.

Peter instantly recognized the shirt. It was bright red with blue Battlebear figures across it. It was Bobby's favorite shirt.

"Bobby!" Peter yelled. He ran straight for his son.

Peter slid to the ground when he reached Bobby. His son was lifeless on the floor. He took Bobby into his arms. Bruises covered his body. Bobby's limbs dangled awkwardly at his side. Footprints could be seen across the boy's chest.

"Help me!" Peter yelled out. "Help me!"

Howard reached Peter. He was already busy calling for an ambulance.

"Help is on the way," he tried to reassure Peter.

"He's going to be okay. He's going to be okay," Peter kept repeating to himself.

Howard did his best to console Peter, but there was little he could do at that point. Bobby was dead. There was nothing anybody could do at that point.

Howard looked up. He saw Jacob still standing

in the same spot at the edge of the clothing department. There was no change in the young man's expression. Jacob was cold. He looked indifferent to his brother's sudden death.

Peter cried over the body of his youngest child. Howard got to his feet. He began to redirect the crowd of customers around Peter.

None of the crowd seemed to notice or care about what was going on. They just wanted around the obstacle so they could continue on with their shopping.

Black Friday had the best deals of the year.

Chapter 2

Five years later

Thanksgiving was cut short for the employees of BestMart. Black Friday was starting at ten o'clock Thursday night. That meant the employees had to be at work even earlier.

The store would be shut down to allow a chance for the workers to set up the new displays for the Black Friday deals. The customers could wait outside in line for their chance to get the new deals.

The break room was packed with BestMart's best and brightest, and everybody else they could hire. It was a sea of purple vests, blue shirts, and khaki pants.

This was the first day for several of the employees. Each one walked in with wide eyes hoping they would recognize somebody from their brief time in training. When they didn't they simply looked for an empty chair next to somebody that appeared friendly.

Lisa approached the entrance to the break room. She took another sip of her soda. She was told her shift was going to last all night. She was going to need all the caffeine she could get.

This was Lisa's first day at BestMart. It was her first job in several months. The last few weeks were especially discouraging as every resume she sent out was ignored and all of her applications were turned down. She was thrilled to finally have a chance to get back to work when BestMart called her. They didn't even want an interview. They sent her straight to training and told her when her first day was going to be.

As Lisa walked into the break room she started to realize she was not the only one whose first day was Black Friday.

"Howdy," greeted Harry. He was the oldest employee at BestMart. He was retired, but proud to say he still worked harder than half the employees there.

"You must be new," continued Harry. "There are a lot of new faces today. Welcome to BestMart."

"Thanks," said Lisa. She took another sip of her soda.

It was a collage of blue and purple from wall to wall. Some faces looked as nervous as Lisa felt. Others were asleep. A couple, Jana and Clark, were busy making out at their table. Lisa tried not to stare at them. As she walked, she passed a table of young women that never took their eyes off of Lisa.

Lisa tried not to pay them any attention, but she could not help it. In the corner of her eye she saw the girl in the center, Jennifer, point at Lisa then giggle with her two friends, Haley and Becky.

There was an empty seat two tables down. Lisa turned away from Jennifer and aimed for her spot. There were already two people sitting at the table. Neither of them was talking and did not look concerned on saving the seat.

"Mind if I sit here?" Lisa asked.

Heather and Taylor looked up from their dazed caffeinated trances. Taylor took one look up and down of Lisa then lowered his head back to the table. Heather was a bit friendlier.

"Go for it," said Heather. Then she zoned back out. Her stare locked onto the wall across the room and it never left.

As Lisa sat down she could still hear whispers coming from Jennifer's table. Jennifer's voice carried through the room. It was difficult to miss.

Curiosity got the best of Lisa. She turned around to see Jennifer and her friends still laughing and looking at Lisa.

Then Jennifer locked eyes on Lisa. Her teasing smile turned into a frown. Jennifer put up one finger and gestured for Lisa to turn around.

Lisa did as she was told. She sat forward in her chair again. The wall was looking like a more pleasant sight every second. She could already feel her first day going downhill.

"Ignore her," said Heather.

"What'd I do?" asked Lisa.

"Nothing. She's the supervisor, and she's a bitch. She's just trying to put people in their place."

Heather never turned away from the wall when she was talking to Lisa. Then without looking she grabbed her cup of coffee and took a drink.

Lisa tried to sneak another look back at Jennifer. It did not go unnoticed.

"Fuck you," whispered Jennifer. Lisa did not actually hear the words, but she could easily understand what Jennifer said.

"I told you to ignore her," said Heather.

"I just want to know what I did," said Lisa.

Taylor started shifting in his chair. He turned his head to look in the direction of Lisa and Heather while still relaxing on his folded arms propped on the table.

"You decided to work here. I think that's grounds enough to be humiliated for. I've done more with less."

"Thanks," said Lisa sarcastically.

Then without hesitation Heather hit Taylor across the back of the head.

"Ow!" cried out Taylor. He straightened up in his chair and rubbed the back of his head where Heather slapped him.

"Fuck you," he said while flipping her off.

"Wake up. Meeting will be starting soon," said Heather.

Then Taylor reached over and took Heather's coffee. He started to chug the lukewarm drink against Heather's protests.

"No, no, no, no, no," said Heather as the last drop went down Taylor's throat.

"Thank you!" Taylor exclaimed.

Lisa watched in silence. She scooted her can of soda to the opposite end of the table from Taylor.

"I'm Lisa, by the way," she said. Lisa hated awkward silences and this one was getting more uncomfortable by the second.

Taylor looked back at Lisa. He leaned forward and eyed her nametag then looked back up at her.

"Yeah… I can read," he said.

"Shut up," said Heather as she shoved Taylor back into his chair. "Hi. I'm Heather."

"Pleased to meet you, I guess this isn't your first day?" said Lisa.

"No," said Heather.

"I have to be honest, I'm a little nervous," said Lisa. "Do they always start people on busy days? I was hoping to start earlier, but they wouldn't let me."

"They only need help for the Christmas season and it doesn't start until today. So it's a lot of people's first day. It's stupid. I know. No offense to you or anything but we're going to be really busy and you don't know what to do."

"I think I can figure it out," said Lisa.

Taylor leaned back into the conversation. His eyes were salivating over the soda Lisa had.

"Lisa, hey, I have a question. In regards to your concerns, of course," said Taylor.

"What?"

"They say one thing that causes jitters is the addition of caffeine into your system. Out of my concern for your nerves, are you going to finish your drink?"

"Fuck you, Taylor," said Heather.

"What? I just don't want to see her drink it and then throw it up an hour later. That would be a waste."

"I think I'll be fine," said Lisa. She grabbed her drink and took another sip. Then when she put it back on the table it never left her hand.

"Have you guys worked here long?" Lisa asked.

"Are you going to be asking questions all day?" asked Taylor.

"Too long," said Heather. She ignored Taylor. It was the best way to deal with him. "I keep meaning to quit. Then my shift starts."

"How hard is it to actually keep your job here? I know I'm only seasonal but they said I might be able to stay on if I do well."

"Dude, this place is Hell," said Taylor. "Get out while you can. Or you'll end up like her." He pointed at Heather. "She's been her for five years, bitching the entire time."

Heather had no problem giving Taylor the

middle finger at his last comment.

"And how would you possibly know that? Oh, that's right; you've been here for seven years. Wait. Make that six and a half. You quit for six months and then begged to come back."

"Yeah… Yeah, it sucks here, but it sucks bigger balls out there. Besides, I can get away with more crap here. Where else can I sleep on the job and call it equipment testing?"

Lisa smiled. "You would rather rule in Hell than serve in Heaven."

Lisa's comment caused Heather and Taylor to stare at her. Heather chuckled. Taylor was left with a look of confusion and awe. Lisa's smile went away. Her comment did not go over as well as she had hoped.

Then Taylor nodded his head and pointed at Lisa with dedication.

"Yes! Exactly. I'm quoting you on that. I'm posting that. You are a wise girl. I like you."

"Thanks, but—" Lisa was cut off before she could correct Taylor on the proper source of her quote.

Richard came marching into the break room. His footsteps were heavy. His shoes had a piece of plastic on their soles that clacked against the tiled floor. He could be heard coming from yards away. Beside him was the assistant manager, Dustin. Dustin stood up straight and tall. His clothes were nicely pressed.

In Richard's hands was a box of donuts made

fresh from the BestMart Bakery. The glaze glistened against the florescent bulbs in the ceiling.

"Quiet down, every one. Quiet down!"

Only Lisa and a handful of others stopped their conversations and turned to address their General Manager. The rest of the employees of BestMart continued on with their Thanksgiving chitchat.

"Quiet down!" Richard yelled again. The louder he was getting was only challenged by his employees.

Then in a fit of rage, Richard threw the box of donuts against the wall. The box burst open and all of the donuts crumbled to the floor.

The spectacle was enough to get the attention of everybody in the room. All eyes were now on their boss and their denied special breakfast.

"What the hell?" Lisa whispered to Heather.

"He has anger issues. You get used to it."

Now that everybody was quiet, Richard cleared his throat and began the speech he had practiced in the mirror fifteen minutes earlier.

"I see a lot of new faces out there. I expect the best out of my older employees. Don't show these new guys shortcuts or any slacking. We need to be at our best. Especially today. It's Black Friday! We'll be opening the doors at ten.

"Like the last couple of years, we'll be trying some new protocols to insure that nothing goes wrong. Safety is our number two priority. Only because our number one priority is our customers!"

"What could go wrong?" whispered Lisa as Richard continued on with his speech about the changes to the register lines and coupon distribution.

"There was an incident a few years back," said Heather.

"What happened?"

"Some kid died!" said Taylor.

"What?!" said Lisa. She could not contain her surprise.

Richard looked up at the three of them. He glared at Heather for a brief second.

"Would you guys shut up," said Heather. She smiled back at Richard.

Then Richard cleared his throat and continued on with his speech.

"We're going to make rope lines for every register that will reach around the store. That way there will be no dispute on who is in what line and they also have the benefit of still shopping while they wait in line!"

Outside BestMart, the line of customers was already reaching around the first corner of the building. Officer Chuck Wilson was near the entrance and was busy directing the newcomers to the back of the line. It became routine after the first few hopeful customers came to the door to start shopping. When he told them where the line was forming they looked at the line then back at him in disgust then back at their fate at the end of the line.

Off in the distance a hooded figure watched the line forming from the parking lot. An older couple brushed past him with little regard. Jacob Adams did not say a word. He kept his eyes on the older couple as the man grumbled about it already being too crowded and they should start Black Fridays earlier.

More cars started to pull in to the parking lot. The brisk cold made everyone move fast to seek shelter against the building. At least they could suffer in line.

Jacob Adams just watched.

"The buddy system is going to be used in order to help keep everything moving smoothly," continued Richard. "We'll designate you a partner for the day later on. You'll be given whistles to call for help from your partner."

Jana snuggle deeper into Clark's arms. "You want to be my partner, babe?"

"Only if you blow my whistle," Clark joked.

Then Dustin stepped forward. He cleared his throat for a professional tone.

"I wanted to speak a little about this year's Black Friday," began Dustin. "The biggest seller is going to be the Battlebears. Battlebears anything. You've seen them on the cookies, the paper towels, soup, and just about everything else. We need to push that. If you are helping a family make sure to present the Battlebear endorsed products. The movie is set to break records. Let's cash in on that. You guy's got it? Be the Battlebear," finished Dustin. He chuckled at his closing line. It was the most popular tagline of the franchise.

Richard stepped back up to finish his presentation. "Thank you, Dustin. Now, I have made a list of groups. Find out which group you are in and get to work on your assigned project. Let's have a great Black Friday, gang! And remember. We're the best Mart!"

Immediately, Taylor stood up as the last hooray for Richard and Dustin. He began clapping as loud as he could. The enthusiasm that Taylor showed rubbed off on the rest of the employees- especially the newer ones. The entire break room started clapping.

Heather tried her best to hold in her laughter. Lisa clapped quietly. She looked over at Richard.

Richard was almost embarrassed at the warm reception he was getting. Dustin was unimpressed, but he kept quiet. He let his eye-roll be his only level of disdain. As Richard started walking out he gave his crew a wave good-bye.

"And somebody clean up those donuts," Richard said before he left the room.

When the door shut behind their managers Taylor finally sat down.

"Ass," said Taylor.

Chapter 3

Jacob watched the line continue to wrap around the building. He stayed hidden in the shadow of a family sized van parked in the middle of the parking lot. The back window had a decal of the family in stick figure form. There were the parents and then a young girl followed by two little boys.

He watched as the line continued to grow restless. Individuals were bouncing on their feet in an attempt to avoid the cold. One group of customers caught the complete attention of Jacob Adams. The older couple that brushed up against Jacob earlier in the parking lot was bickering to each other while in line. Their attention was so focused on their loathing of the cold and the long wait that they did not notice the teenager behind them. The young man's movements were slow, but Jacob had no trouble spotting his plan.

In the line, Sam was standing behind the grumpy couple, John and Blanch. The two had been shopping on Black Friday for years, and they hated it every time. Each year they promised themselves they would never do it again, but each year their granddaughter deserved the next best thing and their daughter-in-law was not going to get up that early to get it for her. John and Blanch believed it was up to them to save Christmas.

The cold was already starting to wear them down. They were getting too old for this. John wrapped his coat tighter around him. Whenever he did that he always made sure not to cover up the logo of his Alma mater. He was proud of his school and his college degree.

"They should let us in now" John grumbled. "They'll make more sales the longer they are open. It makes sense. I'm ready to buy things now."

Blanch reached down to her fanny pack. It was more practical than a purse. She fished around the compartments, moving around several different chapsticks, an inhaler, mints, and loose change. She finally whipped out a packet of disposable hand warmers.

"Here," she presented to her husband. "I told you to take them in the car."

"I don't want them now," said John. "We still have two hours out here. I want them to last."

"Okay, they'll be in here when you want them," said Blanch. She put them pack in the compartment she found them in. "I don't see why you wouldn't want them now. Mine are great."

As the couple continued to argue about the

proper time to start using their resources they did not notice Sam inching his way forward through the line.

The line was condensing. Some patrons up front had given up their spot to try another store. Slowly the line started to move forward, but John and Blanch had not noticed. As they bickered a gap was forming in the line. Sam watched it grow bigger every second.

There were now several feet of open space in front of John and Blanch. Sam looked at it with desire. He watched John and Blanch as they continued to argue about the cold. Eventually the conversation turned to their son and his wife. The longer they talked the more Sam wanted that open spot in front of them.

Sam looked behind him. Nobody was paying attention. They were all in a different world trying to get out of the cold. He looked forward again. John and Blanch still hadn't budged.

Then Sam made his move.

He rocked back and forth on his feet. Each time he shifted slightly closer to the older couple and the open space ahead of them.

Then as casually as he could Sam stepped forward. He moved to the spot in front of John and Blanch and dared not turn around to see if they noticed.

Sam could still overhear the couple talking. He kept his face forward. They hadn't noticed. A smile crept along Sam's face. He was going to get inside that much quicker.

Then he felt a tap on his shoulder.

At first, Sam did not respond. He had committed to his place in line now. He wasn't going to give it up.

"Excuse me," said John while tapping Sam once again.

Sam did not respond. He kept his attention forward.

"Excuse me," said John more forcibly. His tapping was getting rougher. It became more of a shove.

"You cut in line," accused John.

Finally, Sam turned around. He put on a look of confusion to keep up his charade.

"What?" Sam asked.

"You cut in front of us. Get to the back of the line," ordered John.

"I didn't cut in front of anybody. I've been here the whole time," lied Sam.

"No, you were not, you little punk. Get out of line."

"Look old man," said Sam, insulted at the punk comment. "I don't know what the confusion is, but I've been here the whole time."

"Do you want to take this out there?" John asked. He pointed toward the parking lot.

Sam leaned back surprised at the older gentlemen's challenge. He tried to hold back his laughter.

"Dude, I would destroy you. What are you? Fifty? Sixty? I've been here the whole time. If you don't mind please stop talking to me."

"Listen you little snot, I can still open a can of whoop ass."

Their argument was getting louder and drew the attention of everybody in the line around them. Side comments and debates started to spark up about who was right and who was wrong.

"Sir," said a woman down the line. She waved a clipboard with a shopping list above everybody's head to get their attention. "You are right. This guy was behind you earlier. I remember. He must have cut."

"Who asked you?!" Sam yelled at the lady. "Stay out of this, bitch. I didn't cut."

The line grew even louder. They were turning on Sam as he continued to cuss out anybody that disagreed with him. Jacob could hear the whole thing across the parking lot.

"You cut in line. I'm going to get a manager. They're going to kick you out," said the lady with the clipboard.

"Yeah," cheered John. "You're lucky I don't call the police."

"Fine!" yelled Sam. "Shit. I'm leaving. Fuck you guys."

Sam pushed his way out of the line. As he walked away he flipped off everybody around him. The line started to celebrate as they got one more person out of their way.

Sam stomped through the parking lot. He kicked rocks and whatever liter he could at the cars as he passed.

Jacob Adams began to follow him.

Sam's burgundy Pontiac was parked three lanes down from where he was in the line. The lanes were full with cars and there was nobody else walking where he was. He kept cursing the crowd as he returned to his car.

The cold made it hard for him to get out his keys. He had to take off his gloves and when he did his fingers went almost numb. He fumbled around his key ring to get a good grip on his car key to unlock the door.

He didn't notice Jacob approach him until he was right beside Sam.

"Go the fuck away. I'm leaving. You all win," said Sam.

Jacob did not say a word. One arm was forcibly wrapped around Sam's face, and prevented him from screaming. The other swung a hammer straight at Sam's head.

The impact cracked open Sam's skull.

The body spasmed in Jacob's arms then went limp. Quietly, Jacob put the body down on the cold pavement. Then Jacob began looking for the keys to the car.

Chapter 4

Many of the employees of BestMart were huddled together by the communications board in the break room. Richard had posted the list of jobs and groups that were assigned for the day. They all wanted to know what they had in store for the day ahead.

Lisa waited outside the mob of people. She always found it better to wait out the first rush then simply look at the list when the area had calmed down.

Taylor was waiting with her. He had no intention of hurrying up to get to his job. It could wait.

"What happened before?" Lisa blurted out. The thought had been gnawing at her mind since Taylor brought it up during Richard's speech. "You said a kid died."

"Yeah, they managed to keep it pretty hush hush. This fucking place," said Taylor.

"That's horrible," said Lisa.

"It gets worse every year," continued Taylor. He wasn't really listening to Lisa anymore. His answer became more of a ramble of complaints. "Always more people and they are always pissed off. It never stops.

Fucking consumer America and its whores. People die and all they think about is how they could easily survive it. It's bullshit."

"I actually kind of like the idea of it," confessed Lisa.

Taylor stopped what he was saying and looked straight at Lisa with wide eyes.

"How can you like this shit? Sure, fuck my family, but I still like to spread a little Christmas cheer around the holidays. These people want to kill you. It's venomous."

"But isn't that kind of sweet? The hell these people put themselves through just to get a gift for somebody they care about."

"Blah, blah, blah," said Taylor. "It's the thought that counts. I get it."

"Never mind," said Lisa. "You don't get it."

"I just told you somebody died and you're saying it's sweet? What the fuck? That's what I don't get. You are one crazy chick."

Then Taylor looked Lisa up and down one more time. He smiled.

"That's kinda hot," he said.

"That's not what I meant," said Lisa. She gave him a cold stare for hitting on her. "I'm not crazy. Obviously, somebody dying is a horrible thing. I'm just saying in general this kind of—"

Jennifer cut off Lisa. "You need to stop talking

right now. The both of you."

Taylor slumped his shoulders and sighed.

"Hi, Jennifer," he greeted his supervisor with as little emotion as possible. "Whatever do you mean?"

"You know what I am talking about," said Jennifer. "That subject is not to be discussed between the employees. You know that."

"I was just wondering what happened?" Lisa defended.

"Nothing that concerns you," then Jennifer looked at Lisa's nametag to reinforce her statement. "Lisa."

"But what happened?" Lisa asked again.

"I know this is your first day, so I'll make this easy for you. We. Do. Not. Talk. About. It. Next time I hear anything about this I will write you up. Both of you."

Taylor looked away from the confrontation. He was not going to get in the way of Lisa's scolding.

"Okay," said Lisa timidly.

"Good!" triumphed Jennifer.

The three of them stood in awkward silence for a second. Jennifer wasn't walking away. She just stared at Lisa like she was waiting for a reply of thanks.

Then Heather made her way out of the mob of employees with a copy of the lists of jobs.

"Alright I got the list," said Heather. Then she saw Jennifer. "Hi, Jennifer."

"Heather! Great. Mind if I see that?" asked Jennifer. Her cold stare was finally off of Lisa. Jennifer nearly ripped the list out of Heather's hand.

She began to look it over. A frown grew on Jennifer's face as she read the list.

"Tell you what, Heather," said Jennifer. "You can babysit Taylor here. And I'll even give you little Lisa here as well. I'll just put Carl and Marice in another group. You can be the leader! I know you like that."

Then Jennifer handed the list back to Heather. Jennifer's smile once again returned, and it was bigger than ever. Heather was not as thrilled.

"Gee… Thanks, Jennifer. How thoughtful."

"I'm just giving people what they want. See you later, and stop looking at my ass, Taylor."

Then Jennifer walked off. Taylor wasn't listening to Jennifer. He was too busy staring at her ass.

When Jennifer was gone Lisa spoke up.

"Why do I think we just got screwed over?"

"Because we did. No offence to you, but you're new and Taylor is lazy."

"I do my job," Taylor argued.

"Then I expect you to do it. Understood? I'm tired of getting orders from Jennifer. I should be the supervisor and she knows it."

"So what are we doing?" Lisa asked.

"Stocking movies," said Heather as she went

through the revised list in her head that Jennifer declared.

"Yes!" said Taylor as he fist bumped the air. "Jokes on Jennifer, then. I love that."

The employees were released from the break room and sent off to do their assigned duties. Lisa, Heather, and Taylor began to walk down one of the side aisles to get to the entertainment department. Clark and Jana accompanied them.

"Where are you guys heading?" Heather asked.

"No idea. I just follow my man," said Jana as she pulled herself into Clark's arms.

"We are supposed to start putting sales tags on… pretty much everything," said Clark as he looked at his worksheet.

"How did you too get paired together," asked Taylor. "I've been trying to get paired with Trish for months now. They keep saying no because of the one time they found us making out in the bathroom."

"I just traded with Jackson," said Jana. "He wanted to work with Melissa."

"Dammit," said Taylor. "I can't do that. Nobody fucking wants to work with Heather."

"Fuck off," replied Heather.

As the group turned the corner they had to swerve to avoid a wet floor sign left over from earlier in the day. The floor was long dry at this point, but nobody had bothered to remove the sign.

"Hey, Lisa," yelled Taylor. "Slippery when wet!"

Then Taylor shoved Lisa toward the sign. She stumbled forward. The sign went sliding across the floor as Lisa bumped into it. She continued moving forward to regain her balance. But before Lisa could completely get her composure back she ran into their Assistant Manager, Dustin.

Dustin had a cup of coffee in his hands. When Lisa bumped into him he lost his grip on the coffee and it fell to the floor. The scolding hot drink splashed across Dustin's shoes and pant legs.

Lisa looked up at him in horror. She could not say a word. Then she lowered her head. She stared at the puddle of coffee as it spread across the floor.

"Why don't you look where you are going?" Dustin scowled.

"I'm so sorry," she said. "I wasn't paying attention to where I was going. I will clean that up."

"Is there a phone in your hand? No respect from you kids today. How hard is it to avoid walking into another person? What is your name?"

"Lisa. It's my first day," she answered.

"Well, Lisa. Look where you are going next time. You shouldn't have to learn that on your first day. I don't like shenanigans while you are working. The rest of the day should be better than this performance. Clean it up and get back to work."

Dustin then walked off without hearing another thing from Lisa. There was no point.

Lisa held back her tears. It was her first day and already she had been scolded by two of her bosses.

"What an asshole," said Taylor. "Doesn't even offer an apology. If I had a chance I would have told him off."

Lisa looked at Taylor with red, wet eyes. "That was your chance. You missed it."

Then Lisa walked off. She had a job to do. They left Taylor alone to his own devices.

Chapter 5

Howard never bothered to get out of his car. He could keep an eye on the BestMart customer line from his vantage point. It was too cold to start walking around the area and he had to stay in hiding.

He was no longer welcomed at BestMart.

After the incident five years ago the company was ready to brush it aside and continue with Howard as the store manager. They even offered to promote him to the district offices. They told him he did a wonderful job in handling the situation and he was in no way to be blamed. The whole thing was ruled an accident.

But Howard could not focus. He kept replaying the incident in his mind. The boy's death was stuck in his thoughts every day.

It was ruled an accident. But Howard knew differently. He saw Jacob Adams push his little brother into the crowd. Howard tried to deny it to himself at first. He could not believe that anybody would do that to their own family member.

Then as time went on he started to remember the events more clearly. After their father arrived Jacob remained quiet. Howard assumed it was shock. But he never changed.

Howard took an interest in the family. He found himself checking up on them every few days. The company might not have blamed Howard, but he personally did.

Every time he saw Jacob, the young boy was quiet. He stared at Howard with cold eyes. It finally dawned on Howard what was wrong. Jacob never showed remorse for what had happened. He was indifferent.

Then one day Howard confronted Peter about Jacob. He and his wife did not take a liking to Howard accusing their son of murdering their youngest child.

Word got around about the argument, and BestMart fired Howard. There was going to be no promotion, no praise for his job well done. Everything Howard had worked for was gone, because he knew the truth.

Nobody would listen to Howard. The case was closed and they all wanted to put the incident behind them. Howard, on the other hand, could not let it go.

He kept tabs on Jacob over the years. He would search for his name online every now and then. Rarely did Jacob Adams pop up. The teenager kept to himself. A few times Howard started to follow Jacob around. He believed something was wrong with Jacob and he wanted to prove it. But there was nothing.

Howard became a shell of his former self. When he looked in the mirror he no longer recognized his reflection. His beard was unkempt. He could see the despair in his own eyes. He wanted to be out of this obsession he had fallen into, but he could not let go of what he had seen on Black Friday. Bobby' face still haunted him, and there was nothing he could do about it.

Then this year rolled around. A package arrived for Howard a few days before Thanksgiving. It had no return postage. It was crudely wrapped with brown paper and packing tape.

Once Howard got it opened he stood frozen in terror. It was a Battlebear action figure with its head ripped off. It was the same blue Battlebear that was portrayed on the little boy's shirt all those years ago.

Fear consumed Howard. He knew what it meant. The Battlebears were having a resurgence this year. There was a new movie and a new show, and a whole new line of toys coming out. Every child wanted one and parents were going shopping on Black Friday for them.

Jacob knew Howard was looking in on him and now he was teasing the former manager. Jacob was worse than remorseless. He was playing a game. Howard knew something was going to happen this year. He first tried the police, but without any evidence they would not do anything. All he had was an action figure with its head pulled off, and his own word.

Then he called BestMart. First he tried the store itself. Richard was not going to listen. Howard tried the corporate offices later, but they said they could no longer speak with Howard about the matter for legal purposes. He was completely shut off.

That left Howard no choice, but to be a look out for BestMart himself. He arrived early, well before any of the other customers who wanted to wait in line. The day was quiet. There was no sign of Jacob Adams, but as the sun went down Howard started to grow more worried. It was going to be harder to keep track of everything going on.

But he had to try.

Howard picked up his phone. He dialed the number he had written on a piece of paper. This was his third newest phone in two days. He kept changing it to get a new number. Otherwise, nobody would answer his calls.

On the other side of BestMart, Dustin's phone began to ring. He saw the name listed as Unknown Caller. He went ahead and answered it.

"Go for Dustin," he said.

"It's Howard. Do not hang up," Howard pleaded.

"This is my personal number, Howard. How did you even get it?"

"It doesn't matter," said Howard. "You have to

listen to me."

"You cannot be speaking to me, Howard," said Dustin. "This matter has been settled. I am sorry. It's over. Let it go."

"No! You listen to me. Something is going to happen tonight."

"Is that a threat?" accused Dustin.

"Shut up," said Howard. "I got a toy in the mail with its head cut off. It was from Jacob. I know it. I think he's going to attack the store."

"Then take it to the police and they will handle it," said Dustin.

"They will not listen to me," said Howard.

"And neither will I," said Dustin. "You are grasping at straws. I'm sorry for what happened to you. You were great, but this whole thing has destroyed you. I know they deemed you unhirable, but I'm sure if you get your act together we can talk about it in a more formal setting. You just have to be willing to let this go."

The line went dead.

Howard did not have time to listen to Dustin's redemption tactics. The crowd was growing larger with anticipation. Somewhere out there Jacob Adams was waiting for his time to strike. Howard believed that.

Dustin left BestMart through the employee entrance at the back of the store. It was the designated area for all the employees to park and be out of the way for the customers' convenience.

The cold gave Dustin a quick embrace. His pants were still damp from the spilled coffee. Then the assistant manager started his slow journey to his car. He kept his head down to keep his face from the wind. When he started getting closer to his parking spot he finally noticed a burgundy Pontiac parked right behind him perpendicularly. Dustin was completely blocked in.

"What the hell?" Dustin cursed to himself. Luckily the car was still running, and Dustin could see the silhouette of the driver.

"Jackasses," said Dustin as he approached the driver. He could hear music blaring through the car. The radio was turned all the way up.

When he got to the car door, Dustin tapped on the window. The driver did not respond. Dustin tapped again.

"Hey!" he said. He yelled to get his voice louder than the music in the car. The driver still did not respond.

Then Dustin went for the handle. The door was unlocked. Dustin swung it open. The music came roaring out of the car.

"Move your car!" Dustin yelled, but even he could barely hear his own voice over the radio.

Dustin reached over to tap the driver on the shoulder. When Dustin did embrace him, the driver hunched over. His slight touch put the man off balance.

Then Dustin saw it. The gashing head wound on the right side of Sam's head.

"What the hell?" Dustin screamed. It was drowned out by the music.

He never heard Jacob come up from behind.

The first strike was against Dustin's lower spine. The blow from the hammer was strong enough to break its head away from the handle and crack several bones in Dustin's body. Dustin cried out in pain as he crumbled to the ground. Jacob stood over him. Dustin tried to beg for mercy, but he could not be heard over the music.

Jacob stepped down on Dustin's hand. The bitter cold only made the pain worse as Jacob grinned his shoe into Dustin's fingers.

Dustin was pinned against the car. Jacob had him trapped up against the open driver side doorway.

"Please," begged Dustin. His lower back was on fire. He could not walk away even if he wanted to.

Jacob kicked Dustin several more times in the chest. It dropped Dustin lower to the ground. His head rested against the bottom lip of the car. Then Jacob reached for the opened car door.

He slammed it shut.

The door slammed into Dustin's head. Jacob repeated the beating several times. The music waned through the cold winter night every time he struck Dustin.

When Jacob was finished he moved Dustin's body into the car with Sam. The remains of the hammer were discarded in the back seat. Before Jacob left the scene he rummaged through Dustin's pockets. He found the keys to the building.

Jacob Adams made his way to the employee entrance of BestMart. He unlocked the door with ease and went inside. His night was only beginning.

Chapter 6

Richard began his walk through the BestMart. Traditionally he would bring with him a little shopping cart and take a tour around the building. If ever something were misplaced he would put it in his cart and drop it off at its proper location. Tonight he was less proactive and more back seat driver.

"What are you doing?" Richard asked two of his employees at the snack lounge. "Don't put that many chips in one tray. We want this to go as far as we can. We are going to have twice as many customers we usually have."

Richard grabbed an empty nacho tray to show his employees how it was done. He grabbed a small handful of chips and spread them around the empty container.

"Just like that. Got it?" asked Richard. He presented his employees with his wretched display of a nacho tray while he beamed with a proud smile.

The snack lounge was just outside the front entrance to BestMart. Richard could hear the rumblings of the crowd outside. They were growing antsy, but he was not going to open the door until ten on the dot. Those were the rules.

Richard grabbed his mobile work phone and called for the security guard. After a couple of rings Chuck Wilson picked up.

"Hey, Chuck," said Richard. "Can you go out and check on the line again? Just see how they're doing and assure them we'll be open at ten. Thanks."

After Richard hung up he looked back at his two employees making nacho trays. They were still making them wrong.

"I said less chips!"

Harry was working in the backroom of the BestMart. He walked slowly through the supply room and checked over the inventory numbers. The supply room had three main aisles. Shelves were filled with pallets of containers, standees, display pieces, and more.

As Harry walked through the room he would check his clipboard and mark off the boxes that were accounted for. Harry was off two days in a row and whoever was covering his shifts did a poor job. Now, he had to go back and double-check all the work.

The back door to the supply room opened. Harry was not in a position to see who entered. Usually, people used the front door. It was strange, but Harry didn't really bother with it.

"Hello?" he called out. He was curious to see

who came in. They were probably looking for him.

Then Harry began to hear the sound of somebody rummaging through boxes. As fast as he could, Harry started to head toward the source of the sound.

"Stay out of the boxes. I haven't counted everything yet."

The rummaging continued. Harry was almost around the corner. He wanted to catch whoever it was red handed. He was tired of working with untrustworthy coworkers.

Before Harry could reach the end of the aisle the sound was gone. He could hear footsteps walking off. Harry rounded the corner to see the back exit, but the door was already closing. Harry's perpetrator was gone.

The only evidence of tampering was a couple of boxes having been ripped open. One had employee shirts. The other had holiday costumes. Both boxes were tossed and disheveled.

"Damn kids, giving me more work."

Outside BestMart, Howard decided he needed to take a more direct approach if he was going to save everybody from Jacob. He came up to the front entrance of the building where the beginning of the line was waiting.

"All of you guys need to leave. You are all in danger!" Howard shouted.

The crowd stared at him in confusion.

"You're not cutting in line!" said a burly man toward the front of the line.

"No. This isn't about the line. I think somebody is here that wants to hurt you."

"He can bring it," said the man. Then the man flexed his muscles and performed a strong man pose for all to see.

"We can all be in danger," tried Howard again.

"I'm not going anywhere," said the burly man. He was becoming the spokesperson for the line. They all cheered when he spoke for them.

"Please, you have to listen to me," said Howard.

The crowd booed and moaned at Howard's persistence.

"I'm not falling for that shit," said the man. "I'm not running away from anything. I've been here all day. I'm fine."

"You are all going to die!" shouted Howard.

"Whatever," said the man.

The crowd was growing agitated at Howard. The threat of death wasn't settling well with them, but nobody had the courage to step out of line and risk losing their spot.

"Is there a problem here?" asked the security guard, Chuck.

"This guy is trying to scare us all out of here. Probably so he can get the best deals," said the burly man.

"They are all in danger," Howard told Chuck. "You need to listen to me."

"Alright. Alright," said Chuck. He knew Howard from back when Howard was still the general manager. Chuck offered him the courtesy of discretion. "Walk with me, sir. We'll talk away from these people. Tell me what is going on."

Chuck gestured for Howard to follow him out toward the parking lot. They could talk in private and not disturb the rest of the BestMart patrons.

As Howard walked away the crowd began to cheer. They could be in peace once again.

Chapter 7

Lisa, Taylor, and Heather were hard at work setting up a display of one-dollar movies. At least Lisa and Heather were. There were over a hundred titles on sale and each one needed to be readily available and visible for the customers. Taylor was busy reading the back covers' synopsis for each movie he had in his hand.

"Are you going to help us, Taylor?" Lisa asked. She was getting frustrated at her coworker's lack of help.

"Sure, sure. I loved this movie when I was a kid," said Taylor as he put away a copy of Battlebears: Fathoms of War, a film in one of the earlier Battlebear incarnations.

Taylor grabbed the next movie in his bin. As soon as he grabbed it he immediately turned the case around and began to read the back cover.

"Heather, just pass me his movies. I'll get them up," fumed Lisa.

Heather did not hesitate. She took Taylor's bin and slid it over to Lisa. "It's your work."

"Thanks, Lisa!" said Taylor, still reading the synopsis.

"Whatever," said Lisa.

Lisa and Heather continued to work for several more minutes before Richard made his way to their section.

"What is taking you guys so long?" Richard asked as he approached the group. "You should have been done fifteen minutes ago. We have a schedule to keep."

"I'm sorry. There are a lot of movies," said Lisa.

"Don't be sorry. Be faster. This place needs to look perfect and it won't look perfect if there are dvd's scattered like a blind person works here."

"Richard, she's doing her best," said Heather.

"And you guys aren't?" Richard questioned.

Heather fought back the desire to roll her eyes. Richard didn't like her enough as it was.

Then Taylor stepped up.

"Well, Dick. As a matter of fact, no, I am not."

"What did you say?" Richard asked. He eyed down Taylor.

"You heard me... Dick. I'm a little tired. I'm moving a bit slow. Why don't you go get your gal pal, Jennifer, to come do this?"

"You do not talk to me like that. I am writing you up. Do your job or quit."

"Fire me," said Taylor.

Richard and Taylor stood in silence for a moment. Neither of them wanted to budge.

"No," said Richard, finally. "I have a better

idea. You can go clean the bathrooms. I want them spotless. Take all the time you need until we open."

"Fire me," said Taylor.

"Quit or go clean the bathrooms."

Taylor was never going to give Richard the satisfaction of quitting.

"Sir, yes, sir," exaggerated Taylor. He saluted Richard then walked off toward the janitor closet. He had a job to do.

Richard turned back to the girls.

"Get these movies finished," he demanded. Then he walked off to finish his rounds across the store.

"Wow," said Heather once Richard was out of earshot. "You must have really gotten to Taylor. I've never seen him do that."

"I didn't want to get him into trouble. I should go apologize."

"It's okay. Taylor will go dick around in the bathroom for a while and come back right as rain. He was holding us back anyway."

"Sure," said Lisa.

Then the two girls got back to work.

"What are you doing here, Howard?" Chuck asked. Chuck and Howard were alone in the parking lot. They were far enough away from the building that they could talk freely.

"I think Jacob is here," said Howard.

"Why?" Chuck asked.

"I got sent this action figure in the mail." Howard presented Chuck with the beheaded Battlebear. Chuck took it in his hands and examined it.

"It was from Jacob?" Chuck asked.

"There was no return sender," admitted Howard.

"Then how do you know it's from Jacob?"

"Oh come on!" Howard scolded. "Who else would send me a fucking Battlebear? The blue one at that. It was the same Battlebear the kid was wearing when he died."

"I get it," said Chuck. "It is suspicious. But there is nothing to implicate Jacob Adams in this. You are the only one that thinks he killed his brother. The boy is innocent."

"Then why am I getting deranged toys in the mail?"

"It could be a prank," said Chuck. "You haven't exactly made it a secret how you feel about Jacob. Half the employees know the story, and some of them still remember you from your time here. One of them could have sent it to you to fuck with you."

"An employee?"

"We've been selling these things for months," said Chuck. "Anybody could have bought one. It's just a messed up prank. Not everybody liked you, Howard."

"It's not a prank," argued Howard. "I know it

isn't."

"There is nothing you can do," said Chuck. "You have no proof."

"Chuck, please, just keep an eye out," pleaded Howard. "Something is going to happen tonight. I can feel it."

"I will," said Chuck. "Okay? I will keep an eye out for anything suspicious."

"Thank you," said Howard.

"You have to go, now," said Chuck. "You can't be on BestMart property. You know that."

"I know," said Howard. "I'm sorry. I'm just trying to help."

"Thank you," said Chuck. He left it at that. There was not much else he could do to help Howard. The man was obsessed with Jacob Adams.

Howard said good-bye and headed back to his car. He knew when his time was up. He would have to find another way to defend BestMart from its inevitable fate.

Chapter 8

The hardware and automotive section was very quiet. Only one display had to go up involving packages for car accessories. It only took twenty minutes to build and the two employees, Justin and Patrick, spent the rest of their time behind the counter talking about the hotness ranking of all the girls that worked at BestMart. They made it to number six before the debates started to grow heavier.

Their argument over whether Haley was hotter than Claire became so involved they never noticed the stranger walking through their department.

Jacob walked across the back of the aisles of the Hardware Department. He was wearing the familiar blue shirt like all the BestMart employees. His face was now concealed. Jacob Adams wore a reindeer mask with a bright red nose.

His steps were silent as he walked over to the paint section. The aisle was filled from top to bottom with paint buckets. They had every color you could imagine.

Jacob grabbed two buckets of red paint and

continued on his way through the BestMart.

Jennifer and her friends, Becky and Haley, lounged around the changing rooms. Their duties were to monitor the clothes coming in and out of the department to ensure none of the customers stole any merchandise. Luckily, the customers were not inside the store yet.

The three of them sat behind the counter browsing the internet on their phones. Every so often one of them would find a cute picture of a kitten or a funny meme and show the others. Then they would go back to silence and enjoy their connection with the world.

Harry did not care for any of that. He walked straight up to Jennifer to talk to her.

"Somebody is screwing with our inventory," said Harry when he was right up on the counter.

Jennifer did not put down her phone. She merely looked up at Harry. "What?"

"Some kid was going through the boxes before I could count them."

"Did you see who it was? I'll talk to them."

"No. They ran off before I could catch them."

"Then I'll look into it."

"Good," said Harry. "We can't have new people running around like idiots. Do you know how many times I have to look at somebody working here and think how sad it is that this place has gone downhill?"

"Harry, I said I would look into it. Now, we have to get back to work. We're really busy," said Jennifer.

Harry looked at the girls. Becky and Haley were still on their phones. They never once looked up to address Harry when he arrived.

"Thank you," said Harry. Then he walked off. His job was done.

When Harry was gone, Jennifer turned to talk to her friends.

"He always bitches about any little thing," she said. "He makes this job so fucking difficult."

Then Jennifer mimicked Harry's voice, "Back in my day we worked hard."

There was a small chuckle from the group then all three of them went back to surfing the internet.

Taylor propped the bathroom door open as he wheeled in the cart full of cleaning supplies. The mop was always the most difficult task. Its handle stuck out too far, and Taylor had to duck to slide it into the bathroom without getting hit in the head by it.

At first, Taylor began to do his job and mop the bathroom floor. He got several square feet soaking wet before he decided to move on. Taylor looked in every direction to make sure nobody else was in the bathroom. Then he dropped the mop and waltzed into the farthest stall.

Taylor's favorite thing to do was to use the restroom on company time. He dropped his pants down to his ankles and took a seat on the cold porcelain toilet. He really didn't even need to go. He just liked the idea.

He rummaged through his pockets and pulled out a carton of cigarettes. It was too cold to go outside for a smoke break. The bathroom stall would work just fine.

Taylor lit the cigarette and took in a big hit. It felt good. His confrontation with Richard was more nerve-wracking than he thought it would have been. He needed this break.

As he smoked he read the marker graffiti written on the bathroom stall.

John waz here.

For a good time call 555-3933

Jesus watches over us. He is our Big Brother.

Taylor loved reading all the messages. He was responsible for several of them. Then he pulled out his permanent marker and picked a spot for his newest words of wisdom.

I would rather rule in Hell than to serve in Heaven. –Lisa.

When Taylor was done writing he smiled. He was proud of his newest addition.

"I rule this shit, mother fucker," said Taylor.

The door to the bathroom entranced opened.

Taylor huddled down in his spot on the toilet. He leaned forward to peek below the stall doors. All he saw was a pair of feet. Taylor could not tell who it was.

The person walked into the first stall of the bathroom. Taylor followed them closely. Then the person dropped a paint bucket on the floor.

Taylor remained quiet. He didn't want to draw any attention to himself. With his luck it would be one of the supervisors and they would force him back to work, even though he was on a break.

Then a second paint bucket came charging from above into Taylor's stall. It slammed against Taylor's feet. The impact surprised and hurt Taylor. He dropped his cigarette onto his leg. The hot tip caused even more pain for Taylor as he tried to squirm back to composure. It was difficult with his pants around his ankles.

"What the hell, asshole?" cried out Taylor. He looked below his stall, but Jacob Adams was gone. His feet were no longer visible. The only thing Taylor saw was the last remaining paint can.

Then the stalls roared to life. Banging echoed through the bathroom. Taylor looked all around him in surprise. He couldn't see where the sound was coming from.

Then Jacob Adams shadowed over Taylor from the top of the stall. He was like a gargoyle at the top of a building. The reindeer eyes glared at Taylor.

Taylor had no time to react. Jacob jumped down from the top of the stall onto his unsuspecting victim.

The full force of Jacob's body came crashing down onto Taylor's head. His neck snapped back against the metal plumbing of the toilet. Taylor was dead before he could let out a scream.

Jacob opened the stall. His blue shirt was now accompanied by Taylor's purple vest and nametag. There was only a little bit of blood splatter on the shoulder.

He left Taylor's dead body on the toilet. His legs were propped up above the bottom opening of the stall. Then Jacob closed the door and placed an Out of Order sign from the cleaning supply cart on the stall door.

Nobody would disturb Jacob's work. He ventured out of the bathroom and back to the rest of BestMart.

Chapter 9

Lisa and Heather were finally done with their duties at the entertainment section. After they were finished they decided to take a much needed break.

They sat together at one of the tables in the break room. Jana and Clark were at another table in the corner of the room. The two lovebirds were off in their own little world, making out and making an uncomfortable environment for any of the other works that came into the area.

"This is stupid," said Lisa. "We can't finish this list in time while being one man down."

"That's what happens," shrugged Heather. Then she took a drink from her soda that was fresh from the vending machine. "Don't worry about it. We'll be fine."

Jennifer marched into the break room. Becky and Haley closely followed her. Jennifer looked to be on a mission. She eyed Clark and Jana and then looked away in annoyance. Then she set eyes on Heather and Lisa.

"Just the people I'm looking for. I heard you guys got into some trouble earlier with Richard.

Where's Taylor?" Jennifer asked.

"He's in the bathroom cleaning," answered Heather.

"Boys can be so disgusting," said Jennifer.

"What do you want?" asked Heather.

"Somebody has been going through the inventory before it was counted and Harry is having a fuss. I don't want to deal with it. I'm giving the job to you, Heather."

"Thanks," said Heather sarcastically. "Is Harry back there?"

"I don't know. That's your problem now," said Jennifer with a giant smile.

"Don't worry," said Lisa. "I'll help. We can get this done in no time."

Jennifer put up her finger to cut off any of Lisa's ideas.

"Sorry, new girl," said Jennifer. "I have another job for you. I need you to start restocking all the office supplies on the shelf. New strips have come in. They are already in place. You just need to put the product up."

"Isn't that your job?" Heather enquired.

"I'm delegating. I'm trying to get her some more experience. We can't just let the new people stand around. They are only going to learn if they do things for themselves."

"I'll get right on it," said Lisa. She did not want

to fight with Jennifer anymore.

"Great!" beamed Jennifer. Then the three girls left the break room with their heads held high. Jennifer led the way back to their duties at the Clothing Department.

"What did I do to her?" Lisa asked Heather.

"Nothing," said Heather. "I told you. That's just what she does. We better get to work. She'll be back around."

"Can't you just report her?" asked Lisa.

"All the managers think she's great. They won't listen to us. Just get used to it for the next few weeks. Alright?"

"Just because you are used to it doesn't mean it's okay," said Lisa. She was growing agitated. Her whole day was a wreck and there was no sign of it getting any better. "I want to actually enjoy the place that I work, and I already hate it here. It's one piece of bullshit after another."

Then Lisa turned to Clark and Jana in a fit of rage. The sound of the smacking of their lips was overbearing. "Would you please find a room?!"

Clark and Jana tore away from each other for a brief moment to glare at Lisa.

"Fine," said Jana. "Let's get out of here. We have to work to do anyway."

Clark and Jana got up. Jana held her head high in defiance of Lisa as she left the break room. Clark held back for one second.

Then he turned to Lisa and Heather.

"If I don't get laid today because of you..." he begrudged.

"Just keep walking," said Heather.

Then Clark was gone.

"Lisa, you have got to lighten up a bit. I can't keep defending you," said Heather.

"I don't need protection," said Lisa. "I have more work to do."

Chapter 10

Howard was not satisfied with his last conversation with Chuck Wilson. Chuck was a good guy, but Howard knew he ultimately didn't take Howard seriously.

Howard drove around to the back of the store where the employee parking was held. Nobody was in the area so Howard parked his car and decided to poke around.

Dustin's car was still in the parking lot. Howard would never forget the SUV that Dustin drove. It always smelled like smoke and pizza.

Howard was going to have to be careful. There were still a handful of employees that could recognize Howard from when he worked at BestMart years ago, even with his scruffy beard.

The former manager approached the employee entrance to BestMart. Howard was not surprised to find the door still slightly open. The door never latched properly. Until it was sealed tightly shut, the door was never truly locked.

Howard opened the door with ease. Once he was inside he shut the door properly. He didn't want any unwelcomed guests.

He journey through the back hallways of the store. They had changed nothing since his last day. The only difference was the organization. Richard didn't have any and didn't enforce it with the employees.

The first thing Howard did was head straight for the supply room.

Howard grabbed a blue shirt and purple vest, and put them on over his clothes. He needed to blend in. As long as he could avoid the employees who knew who he was he could roam through the building freely.

Before he left the supply closet, Howard looked around. The coast was clear. Howard took a deep breath then he began his journey through BestMart on his hunt for Jacob Adams.

Lisa was alone on her newest duty. An entire pallet of paper and office supplies waited for her in the aisle. The shelves were bare. Lisa had to hunt down where each product went. The only reference was matching the barcodes on the product to the codes on the shelf. It was time consuming for her since she had no idea what the layout was supposed to look like.

After the first few products made their way onto the shelf, Lisa was starting to get the hang of it. She was remembering numbers and abbreviated names for the products and was able to find holes more quickly. She was well on her way.

Out of the corner of her eye, Lisa saw somebody walk past the aisle. She stopped what she was doing to get their attention.

"Hey! Hey! Can you give me a hand?" she called out.

There was no reply.

Lisa stood up to follow her coworker. She was getting tired and as much progress as she was making she knew she needed help.

She turned the corner to find the main aisle empty. Then Lisa looked to her right to look into the aisle next to her. She caught the back of Jacob Adams as he walked toward the next aisle.

Lisa followed. She was getting ticked off at having to play chase.

Jacob Adams stopped in the office supply area. He peered at the guillotine papercuter that was on display. He unlatched the blade and held it in his hand.

"Could you help me?" Lisa asked again. She finally caught up to Jacob in the aisle. He was down at the other end, but she could see him with his back to her. Jacob's newest weapon was hidden from view.

Jacob did not reply.

Then Jacob began to walk off again.

Lisa gave up. She didn't want to waste anymore time trying to find help.

"Fine! Don't work here either," she grumbled.

Then Lisa got back to work.

Howard walked into the employee break room. There was no sign of Jacob, only Jennifer, Becky, and Haley. The three girls were taking a break while playing games on their phones.

Howard did one last double take around the room before Jennifer took notice of him. She looked at her two friends.

"Watch this?" she said. Then she got up from her chair. She started to walk over to Howard.

"You're late," she said.

Howard stopped looking around and turned to Jennifer. He was surprised to see her as a supervisor. She wasn't around for very long by the time Howard left BestMart, but he was never impressed with her work ethic when they did work together.

"What?" Howard asked.

"You're late," repeated Jennifer. "We had the meeting over an hour ago. I didn't see you there."

Jennifer got closer to Howard. She was breaking into his personal space.

"Who hired you anyway?" Jennifer asked. She picked at Howard's shirt. "You look like a mess."

"Please back away from me," said Howard.

"Why? Something the matter?"

"I'm really busy," said Howard.

Jennifer got even closer to Howard. He could feel her breath on his face. Haley and Becky giggled in the background.

"Doing what? You just got here. You know BestMart doesn't take too kindly to a nasty beard like yours," she said. Jennifer proceeded to rub her hand across Howard's face. "But I like it. I like older men."

Howard grabbed Jennifer's arm and pulled her hand away from his face. Then he stepped back a couple of steps.

"I said get away from me. I have things to do," said Howard.

"Don't touch me," Jennifer scolded. "That's sexual harassment. I can get you fired. You're mine now, you piece of shit. You do what I say or I'll report you."

Howard glared at Jennifer. He was unimpressed with her tactics.

"Grow up," said Howard.

Then Howard turned away from Jennifer. She did not worry him.

"Come back here," ordered Jennifer.

Howard was not listening. He continued to walk out of the break room. He still had to find Jacob.

"Come back here!" Jennifer demanded. Before she could say it again Howard was gone. When she turned around Becky and Haley were staring at Jennifer. Jennifer fumed.

"What?" asked Jennifer. "Get back to work."

Clark and Jana were in the Baby Department. They had several items they needed to re-price for the Black Friday sale. The two of them worked shoulder to shoulder as they put new price tags on all the items.

"Do you know what all these diapers make me think of?" Clark asked Jana.

"Please, don't say some stupid fart joke."

"Nope," Clark said. He looked Jana in the eyes and raised his eyebrows with interest. "Making babies."

Then Clark slapped his girlfriend's ass.

Jana let out a little cry from the attention then leaned in close. She kissed Clark. He kissed her back. Then they started making out.

"That's enough," said Jana as she pulled away from Clark. "We're not going to be making babies here."

"Oh, come on, baby," teased Clark. "I'm sure you'd be a wonderful mother to some baby."

Clark kissed Jana again. He accompanied it with a grope of her breast.

"No," said Jana. "We're out in the open. There should be some place we draw the line."

"Isn't that the fun of it? Nobody will catch us... or will they?"

Clark went in for another kiss. Jana kissed him back with more passion.

"Make it quick," said Jana.

"Like always," Clark joked.

Clark wrapped his arms around Jana. He kissed

her down her neck. First, he took off Jana's vest. Then he unbuttoned her shirt one button at a time.

"Back here," Jana said as she gestured for them to go to the back of the aisle.

"In the back? Alright," Clark cheered.

Jana glared at Clark for a moment because of his stupid joke then beckoned for him to come closer.

Clark embraced her again. They started making out and were only paying attention to each other and their needs.

They did not notice Jacob Adams approach them.

The first swing of the papercutter struck Jana across the back of the neck. The blade cut into her vertebrae. She never felt the blow. Blood gushed out of her wound. It poured down her and Clark's chest.

Clark took a second to realize that Jana was no longer moving. He looked into his girlfriend's dead eyes.

Then Jacob came from behind and slid the papercutter across Clark's throat. Clark could not scream. His airway was clogged with blood.

Both the bodies fell to the floor. Jacob leaned down and hacked away at their bodies several more times. Blood spilled out onto the floor in a puddled mess.

Finally, Jacob Adams stood up and admired his work. Clark and Jana were dead in each other's arms; their final embrace.

Chapter 11

There was still a quarter of the pallet left for Lisa to finish. The shelves were mostly full, and Lisa was having an easier time filling the holes that were left. Her back was starting to hurt from the constant bending and lifting. Boxes of reams of paper were not light.

As she grabbed the next box of paper from the pallet another coworker came walking by. Lisa hesitated, but once again attempted to get their attention for some help.

"Can you help me?" Lisa asked.

Howard looked over at Lisa. He barely noticed her when he was walking by.

"What was that?" he asked.

"I can use some help," said Lisa. "If you don't want to then whatever. You're not the first to ditch work."

"Sorry," said Howard. He walked over to Lisa. He took the box of paper that she was going to grab. "I'm just looking for somebody."

Howard carried the box over to its spot on the shelf. He didn't even think twice about putting it on the shelf. It was second nature still.

"Thanks," said Lisa. "Who are you looking for?"

"His name is Jacob," said Howard. "He doesn't actually work here."

Lisa grabbed another box of paper and walked over to Howard. She started putting the new product on the shelf.

"If he doesn't work here then what is he doing inside?" Lisa asked. "We're not open yet."

"I'm just double checking," said Howard. "He's done some vandalizing. You never know, really. If you see anybody causing trouble then get security. Or me if I'm around. We'll take care of it. Don't confront him yourself."

"Is he dangerous?" Lisa asked.

"I hope not," said Howard. "I just want to be cautious."

Howard finished up his box of paper products. "I'm sorry, but I have to be going. I need to keep looking. Sorry, I couldn't help more."

"No, it's okay," said Lisa. "Thanks for the help."

Howard left Lisa to continue her job. As he walked he checked every aisle that he passed. So far he had not found any sign of Jacob Adams.

Richard continued his rounds around the store. This was his third lap. Things were progressing at a slow rate. His employees needed to step it up. Some days he wished he could do away with all of them and hire all new employees. Ones he could train himself and they wouldn't adapt any of the crappy habits the older crew picked up.

He walked into the Baby Department to see how Clark and Jana were doing. To his surprise and disgust, neither of his employees were there and they left a giant puddle of red paint spilled all over the floor. The paint bucket was popped open and crushed. Paint was slowly leaking from the container.

"Oh, this is ridiculous," said Richard. "What is paint doing in the baby aisle? I work with a bunch of animals."

Richard stormed off.

He found Jennifer in the break room. She was going over the daily schedule while Becky and Haley were on their phones.

"Jennifer," said Richard. As soon as the girls heard Richard's voice they all scrambled to attention. Becky and Haley immediately put their phones away and tried to make it look like they were intently listening to instructions given to them by Jennifer.

"How is everything going?" Richard continued.

"Fine, Richard," said Jennifer. "Just planning for the rest of the day. How do you feel about putting Heather on elf duty? She's great with kids."

"Whatever you think would work. Also, there is a spill in the Baby Department. I need you to clean it up. When you find Clark and Jana also, write them up, and show them how to properly clean up their own messes."

"No problem," said Jennifer. "I'm on it."

Richard did not say another word. He left the girls in the break room. He had to get back on his route. The store was not going to be ready on its own.

"Haley," said Jennifer when Richard was gone. "Go mop up the spill."

"But he said for you to do it," Haley complained.

"I don't care what he said. I'm your boss. Do it."

Haley stood up and stormed off. She was not going to argue any further.

Jennifer turned to Becky. "She is so lazy some times."

"I don't know how you put up with her," said Becky.

Jacob Adams stalked through the front lobby of the BestMart. He dispassionately walked across the front entrance in full view of the crowd outside in the front of the line. They banged against the window eager to get inside and start saving.

Jacob ignored the crowd and walked to the HR office. The door was locked but he had the keys to the entire building. Jacob let himself in and disappeared behind the door.

Haley sulked as she mopped up the paint that was spilled all over the baby aisle. She never bothered to pick up the paint bucket. Every time she brushed her mop across the floor Haley would knock the paint bucket and it would release more of the paint that was still left over in the canister. It created an endless cycle as Haley continued to spread the dark red paint across the floor.

As Howard walked through BestMart his eye caught the bright red on the floor. He stopped to see Haley continuing to fail at her job.

"Stop," he said. "Wait. What happened?"

"Some douche spilled some paint," said Haley.

"Are you sure it's paint?" Howard asked. He knelt down to take a closer look at the spill.

"Are you blind, man? You do see the paint bucket there, don't you? It's paint."

"But why is there paint here?"

"I don't know. I'm not Google. Stop asking me questions. Shit."

"You don't care at all about this?"

"No," said Haley. "I don't. This place can suck it. I do all the work around here."

Haley put her head down and went back to mopping. She was tired of this job already.

Howard looked around. He looked for any further clues to the origin of the paint spill. There was nothing. Haley was no help, so he continued on with his search.

Jacob Adams never bothered to turn on the lights to the HR office. His secrets were hidden in that room and attention could not be drawn there.

The only source of light was from the monitors on the desk in the back of the room. They showed footage from all of the video cameras in the building.

Jacob watched as Howard walked away from Haley and continued on his walk through BestMart.

Then the reindeer face turned its attention to another screen. Jacob Adams watched Richard as the general manager was looking over the cash registers in the check out area nearby.

Chapter 12

Lisa finally made it to the last box on her pallet. She was thrilled to see the end. All that was left were some pencils, and she knew exactly where they went. There was only one open spot left.

As Lisa put the last few packages on the shelf Jennifer came by to check on her progress.

"You are doing this all wrong," Jennifer gasped.

"What?" Lisa asked, stunned.

"You are doing this completely wrong. Didn't you look at the display plan?"

"What display plan?" asked Lisa. "I never saw a display plan. There wasn't one. I've just been putting stuff where they belong on the shelf according to the strips."

"Well, if you had looked at the display plan like you were supposed to you would have noticed that the strips are wrong."

Lisa looked wide-eyed at Jennifer then at the strips then back at Jennifer.

"You said they changed the strips? How is this wrong?"

"It looks like somebody didn't do their job on the reset. The strips weren't changed. You should have checked that before you starting stocking all these items. You'll have to get the new strips and place everything in their proper spot. You're wasting all of our time, Lisa. Apparently, Heather hasn't taught you anything."

"Nobody told me about any display plan," said Lisa. "I didn't know. I can't do this on my own. I need help. Please."

"Fine," said Jennifer. "I can only help for a second. I'm very busy today. We all are, and mistakes like this cost us all."

Jennifer stuck her hand deep into the shelf of pencils Lisa was near. Then in one motion she pulled on a package of pencils from the back of the row. It forced all of the pencils on that peg to fall out to the floor in the aisle. Fifteen packages of pencils spilled out onto the floor at Lisa's feet.

"There you go," said Jennifer. "You can start there. I have to go now. I'll be back soon to check on you. Find the new strips. You need to get this fixed before we open."

Lisa started picking up the supplies while Jennifer walked off.

Heather was busy going through the inventory in the supply room. Harry was nowhere to be found. She only found his clipboard when she arrived in the storage room. She always thought his notes were those of a madman. She could barely read his chicken scratch handwriting and he always did his addition in the margins creating more chaos of numbers than what was necessary.

She began going through the supplies and tried to make sense out of Harry's notes. Even with the lights on it was still rather dark in the room. The shelves were high enough to block out much of the light in between the aisles.

"Damn it, Harry," cursed Heather. "Is this a four or a nine? Not that it matters because there are six of them."

Footsteps shuffled across the room. Heather looked up from her work. She tried to peer through the shelves, but she could not see who entered the room.

"Harry?" she called out.

The footsteps continued. They were heading toward her.

"Harry, is that you?" she asked. There was still no reply.

Heather began to walk toward the sound. She needed help with the paperwork and if Harry was finally back she could get some actual work done.

"You deaf bastard," Heather whispered to herself. "Harry! Whoever!"

Then out of the shadows she saw the familiar blue and purple. Then Harry came grumbling into the light.

"What? You don't have to yell," said Harry.

Heather was relieved to see Harry finally.

"Where have you been? I've been doing the inventory forever. I need your help."

"I took a little break," said Harry.

"I've been here for an hour," said Heather.

"I'm not as young as I used to be," said Harry. "If I were, I could work circles around all of you."

"Yeah, yeah," said Heather. "What's wrong with the inventory?"

"Some kid was going through the North Pole display. I don't know what all he took. And some of our shirts."

"Okay," said Heather. She sounded defeated. She was counting other items for very little reason then. "That shouldn't be too bad to go through. Show me what happened."

"Harry turned around and gestured for Heather to follow her.

"They are over here. A bunch of hooligans. That's who did it. Can't find good help anymore."

Harry continued on with his ramblings. Heather zoned it out. She just wanted to get this done and get back to real work.

Chapter 13

Jacob Adams stood in the corner of the front entrance of BestMart. He looked over at the line of customers waiting to be let in. The image of a man in a reindeer mask reflected off of the glass. His newest weapon dangled in his hand.

Then his attention turned toward the cash registers. He saw Richard fumbling around checkout stand number eight.

Richard hurriedly realigned the ropes that made the barrier for the lines at the registers between eight and nine. The register drawers were almost counted and soon BestMart would be open. He wanted to make sure everything was perfect when it was.

As he continued his inspection he noticed one of the signs on the register was crooked. He reached over to straighten it.

"Lazy kids," muttered Richard. "How hard is it to get something straight?"

Richard took his hand away. The sign was level. Then it shifted back down to its original awkward position. Richard frowned.

"They can fix it later," he said.

Jacob walked across the registers. He caught Richard's attention.

"Hey! Hey!" Richard called out. "Come back here."

Jacob continued walking. He turned into the Jewelry Department. Richard followed.

"You might as well stop now," said Richard. "I will catch you. Then you will be in trouble. So if you are smart you might as well stop now."

Jacob stopped. He turned around and faced Richard. The reindeer mask stared at the General Manager.

"Oh, how cute," said Richard. "Now, I have no idea who you are."

Then Richard looked down at Jacob's nametag. "Taylor."

Jacob did not move. He hid his blade behind his back, out of view of Richard.

"That is it," said Richard. "You win. You are fired. You can go home. We'll mail you your check. And you're paying for that mask."

Jacob attacked Richard.

He shoved the papercutter into Richard's oversized gut. Richard screamed out in pain and terror. Jacob was unable to cover Richard's mouth. Then Richard fought back. He swung wildly. One shot grazed Jacob's face. The mask was knocked out of place.

It blinded Jacob for a moment.

He swung his blade in the air, but missed Richard. Richard took the time to stumble away from his attacker. Blood left a spotted trail behind Richard as he made his escape.

Jacob recomposed himself. He settled his mask over his face properly. Then he watched as Richard attempted to flee. Richard was going for the main doors at the entrance of BestMart. Jacob started to follow.

The crowd outside watched as Richard made his way to the sliding glass doors. He was nearly hunched over holding his stomach. The crowd grew excited as Richard got to the doors. They cheered and hollered that they were going to be let in early.

Richard pulled out his keys. He kept looking backward. Across the lobby Jacob Adams was approaching. Richard moved faster with his keys. He needed to escape. He needed to get away from the man with the knife.

Richard found the right key. He put it in the lock and began to unlock the door. The crowd grew restless. They pressed up against the door. The greatest sales of the year were waiting for them.

Jacob slowly paced toward Richard and the front entrance. Blood dripped off of Jacob's blade.

"Jacob?"

Jacob paused. He looked behind him. Howard was standing just beyond the front entrance. He looked at Jacob dead in the eyes.

Then Richard opened the sliding glass doors. He only got a few inches before the crowd outside took it from there.

The greedy mob charged forward. They had no further regard for Richard. They trampled over the injured general manager as they made their way into the BestMart.

Noise erupted through the building as the crowd cheered and celebrated to be out of the cold. The mob swarmed through the front lobby. Jacob was lost in the chaos. Customers didn't pay him any attention as they surrounded him and charged right past him.

The mob rushed forward. Howard tried to fight against the current, but every step he moved forward he was pushed back three. He could not get anywhere close to where Jacob was.

"Jacob! Jacob!" Howard yelled. "Move!"

It did no good. The harder Howard fought the crowd the more they fought back. The customers were too eager to get inside and start shopping. Nothing was going to stand in their way.

Howard looked back toward the front entrance. Jacob Adams was gone.

Chapter 14

Lisa had abandoned her task in the paper and office supplies aisle. She never found the new strips. Instead, she put the pencils back on the shelf that Jennifer was kind enough to take down. Then she found a new project to help with in the home décor section.

She was busy folding towels when a customer rushed by the aisle.

Then another.

Then another.

Lisa walked out to the main aisle to get a better look. She saw the herd of customers coming her way. She looked down at her watch. It was only 9:30. The store was opened early.

"Oh, no," said Lisa.

Heather was in the break room. She was finally done helping Harry with the inventory. It was a chore to keep Harry focused on the job at hand. He always wanted to talk about one thing or another. He was easily distracted.

She was finally glad to have a moment to herself.

Soon she would have to go back to work, but for those few minutes she could relax.

Then Heather heard the commotion out in the store. Her curiosity got the better of her. It should not have been that loud out there.

She opened the door of the break room and looked out to the store. Her eyes grew wide in fear. They were open.

Jennifer, Becky, and Haley were back at their posts in the Clothing Department. The swarm of customers rushed past the department. The girls looked up from their phones. They saw the swarm of customers start looking around for the best deals in the store.

"What are you all doing here?" Jennifer panicked.

The crowd was too loud. Nobody could hear Jennifer over their own voices. Becky and Haley were stunned silent. The two girls ducked down under the counter.

"We're not open!" Jennifer yelled out. "We're not open!"

The Black Friday shopping experience was beginning all across the store. Fights were already starting to break out between customers.

Howard pushed his way through the furious crowd. He ignored several attempts from customers to get his attention. He was constantly on the lookout for Jacob.

Two customers bumped into him. They were too busy arguing to notice Howard was in their way. Howard could barely think. There was too much going on around him.

"Go find your own Max Menacer!" shouted one of the men.

"Ha ha! I got the last one!" said another.

Howard continued to cut a path through the customers. There was still no sign of Jacob Adams anywhere.

Heather led an army of BestMart employees to the registers. They each carried a tray of money.

"Okay, everyone, get to your stations!" she ordered. "Get your registers ready as fast as you can. I don't want any messing around."

They all nodded their heads. One by one Heather rushed to each register and opened the drawers so the employees could put the money away.

There were already people in line ready to check out. Heather rubbed her temples. She was developing a major headache.

"Where the hell is Richard?" she wondered out loud.

Becky and Haley stayed hidden underneath the

counter. Jennifer was stuck behind it as half a dozen customers were all fighting for their questions to be answered first. Jennifer froze in shock.

"Where can I find the big screen TVs?"

"I saw this movie cheaper at another store. Will you match the price?"

"I accidentally stepped on this. Is it cheaper now because it's damaged?"

Lisa rushed forward through the crowd. She approached Jennifer behind the counter of the dressing rooms.

"What is going on?" Lisa asked. "What happened?"

Lisa hated having to ask Jennifer for answers, but Jennifer was the first supervisor she saw. It was her only choice to get answers.

Jennifer stared back at Lisa. "Um... um... help these customers!"

Then Jennifer was off. She walked away as fast as she could through the crowd of people. Jennifer no longer even tried to answer any questions. One customer held up a dvd to Jennifer's face, but Jennifer put up her hand and continued walking away. She could not deal with the situation.

Heather tried for the third time to get a hold of Richard. He was not answering his managerial phone or his personal cell phone. The phone simply kept ringing.

“Pick up, Richard!” Heather yelled into the phone.

Finally, she gave up. Heather slammed the phone onto its dock.

“Fine! Looks like I’m in charge then. God, help us all.”

Chapter 15

Howard forced his way through the crowd. Every few feet he would stop and take another look around him. He could not find Jacob Adams anywhere in the mob of people.

The crowd began to tighten around him. He was getting squeezed in.

Then he started having flashbacks. His mind raced to five years ago. The crowd was uncontrollable then. He relived watching the young boy get trampled by the mob of unruly customers. Then he saw Jacob Adams' face. He showed no emotion as he looked at his little brother's lifeless body. Howard relived the moment in his head. He saw Jacob push the little boy into the crowd. It was clear as day.

A shiver went down Howard's spine. He had to find room to breathe. Howard was near the Clothing Department. He rushed over to one of the circular racks of hanging shirts.

Howard ducked through the clothes and found solace in the middle of the rack. It was a small space, but there was nobody else there. He could relax and compose himself.

After a moment of deep breaths, Howard stuck his head over the top of the rack. He looked out at the sea of customers surrounding him. There were faces everywhere, but no sign of a reindeer mask.

Then Lisa poked her head into the clothes rack.

"What are you doing in here?" she asked.

Howard let out a little scream. He did not see her coming.

"Whoah, don't do that," he said.

"Sorry," said Lisa as she stepped inside the clothes rack with Howard. "But again, what are you doing in here?"

"Hiding," said Howard. "Too many people."

Lisa laughed. "You can't just hide. What are you afraid of?"

"Nothing," lied Howard. "I just don't like crowds."

"It's your job to deal with this place. Suck it up and get out there."

"No," said Howard. "You don't understand. Just get out of here."

"What the hell? Why is everybody here so lazy? Just do your job."

"I have other things to worry about, alright."

"Do what you want," said Lisa. "Is that right? Is that the motto here? Just let things go and do what you want?"

"Just go away," said Howard.

Lisa stared down Howard.

"I'm getting back to work," she said. "I could use your help. I can't do this alone, and Jennifer already abandoned me."

Then Lisa left the clothes rack.

Howard took a few more breaths then looked back up out of the rack to see the crowd. He still did not see Jacob Adams, but he knew the killer was out there somewhere.

Outside the BestMart by the employee parking lot, Haley was enjoying an overdue smoke break. She leaned against the wall and let in another breath of smoke and nicotine. She was lucky to have gotten away from the angry mob. Jennifer had already ditched them, which was typical.

The entrance back inside was propped open with a small rock. As much as she wanted to, Haley did not want to get locked out. Then the door opened.

Jacob walked out into the cold. The antlers on his reindeer mask brushed in the wind.

Haley relaxed a bit as Jacob walked out. She was relieved.

"I thought you were going to be Jennifer," she said.

Jacob stayed quiet and stared at Haley.

"Ho ho ho," she laughed. "Is Richard making

you wear that?"

Jacob did not say a word.

"What? Fuck you, Taylor. Alright? Go away, and don't tell anybody I'm out here."

Jacob remained where he was.

"Just don't stand there," begged Haley. "It's giving me the creeps. Asshole. I just wanted to take a break in peace for a second."

Jacob looked Haley up and down. He tilted his head back and forth.

"Fuck off," said Haley. She flicked her cigarette at him. The cigarette butt hit Jacob on the chest then fell to the ground.

Haley didn't waste any time. She quickly got out a new cigarette and lit it up.

Jacob started to walk toward her.

"What?"

Jacob reached out and grabbed Haley by the throat. The cigarette fell out of her mouth.

Jacob stabbed her in the stomach. He sliced across her belly. She cried out in pain before falling to the ground.

Jacob towered over her. She looked up at him through teary eyes.

Jacob knelt down. He picked up the cigarette that Haley just dropped. It was still burning hot.

He grabbed hold of Haley's face. His hand held her head down against the pavement by covering her mouth. Then he forced the cigarette into Haley's eye.

She tried to cry for help, but Jacob gagged her with his hand. Then Jacob began to slice her several more times with his blade.

Chapter 16

Lisa was kept busy in the Clothing Department. Her latest customer was an older lady that asked for a shirt from the top shelf. Lisa was more than happy to oblige.

She reached up and grabbed the red shirt the old lady asked for. The shirt had a collage of marijuana leaves sprinkled across it.

"Thank you dear," said the old lady. "That was very nice of you."

"No problem," said Lisa. "Here you go."

"My grandson will love this shirt. That's his favorite color, you know."

"It's a nice color," said Lisa. She smiled back at the lady.

Then she felt a forceful tapping on her shoulder. Lisa turned around. Blanch greeted her with a look of disgust on her face.

"Excuse me," said Blanch.

"Yes?"

"Is there any order in this place? This thief stole my music player from my own cart!"

Blanch pointed towards a young girl with several tattoos presented down her arm. The girl, Renee, noticed she was being pointed at and decided to confront Blanch about the accusations.

"Don't listen to her. I didn't steal anything," said Renee.

Blanch charged forward to come face to face with Renee. Lisa tried to get in between them.

"I can tell you are lying. I had that very box in my cart and I turned around to find you holding it, punk!"

"I got this one from the shelf. I didn't take anything from your stupid cart, lady."

"Ladies, please, let's discuss this without fighting," suggested Lisa.

"Tell her to give me back my music player," demanded Blanch.

"I didn't take your music player. And this is called an mp3 player. Get it right. You shouldn't even be allowed to have one if you don't know what it's called."

"Enough!" Lisa shouted. Then she turned to Blanch. "Now, ma'am, unfortunately I can't just take somebody's word over the other's without hearing the story. Did you actually see her take the mp3 player?"

"...No. She was standing right by my cart with it in her hands. She stole it!"

"You did not see her take your mp3 player. You

don't actually know it was her."

"You are going to side with her!" Blanch announced. "All you young kids are gangbangers. You two need to find Jesus before it's too late. What's your name?"

Just then Heather cut into the argument. She could hear it a dozen yards away.

"Her name is Lisa, and she is doing her job. Ma'am, if you had not stopped to accuse this girl of stealing you probably could have gotten yourself another mp3 player as they were still on the shelf just a minute ago. But because of this useless rant you are going on you are out of luck. Enjoy the rest of your shopping experience."

By the end of Heather's speech she was face to face with Blanch. Heather was not backing down.

"I am never shopping here again," Blanch declared.

"I look forward to it," said Heather with a smile.

"I am going to write a letter to your manager about you two. You two are going to be fired."

With Blanch's final words she ditched her cart where it was in the Clothing Department and stormed off.

Renee turned to Heather. "Thanks," she said.

"Did you steal it?" Heather questioned.

"No!" Renee reinforced.

"Just checking," said Heather.

Then Renee stomped off ticked that she was still accused of being a thief.

When the coast was clear Lisa hugged Heather.

"What the hell was that?" Lisa asked.

"I don't know," said Heather. "I've lost it. This is crazy."

"Tell me about it. I thought we weren't opening for another half an hour."

"That's what I thought too. Nobody was ready and Richard didn't even have the courtesy to tell us. I can't get a hold of him or Dustin or anybody. They won't answer their phones."

"What about Jennifer? Have her deal with this," said Lisa.

"I haven't seen her," said Heather.

"She was here earlier. Then she stormed off and told me to deal with it," said Lisa. "I guess I shouldn't be surprised."

"If you see her again tell her I'm looking for her. Until then, I'm in charge."

"Sounds good," said Lisa. "What would you have me do?"

"Just keep doing what you are doing. Help customers with what they need. And if you see Taylor, tell him I want to see him."

"You got it."

Jacob walked through the crowd. He was

pushing a dolly with a heavy plastic container through the crowd. He ignored every customer around him and forced his way through. People either got out of the way or were shoved out of the way. The wheels of his dolly rolled over feet as it went by. Customers complained and argued but nobody stopped the masked man.

As he made his way through the crowd, Jacob brushed past an unsuspecting Lisa. Lisa was too distracted to give him too much attention.

She made a quick glance in his direction. For a second she thought it was weird that a guy with a mask was wheeling a container through the crowd, but then a customer pulled her away.

"Excuse me," asked the older woman with cats on her sweater. "How much is this? The ad said it was $49.99."

Howard found himself in the Toy Department of BestMart. He kept his eye out for Jacob while he got on his phone. The Battlebears were flying off the shelf. Several customers asked Howard for help in finding more Battlebear actions figures, but Howard kindly ignored them. He was too busy waiting on hold to deal with any of the customers.

"Thank you for calling BestMart. Sorry about the wait, how can I help you?" said the representative at the customer service desk.

"Yes, hi," said Howard. "I need you to get a hold

of Chuck Wilson. He's the officer on duty. I'll hold. Just find him. I want to speak with him."

As Howard was waiting for the BestMart employee on the other end of the phone to connect him to Chuck, John approached Howard with a customer question.

"Sir, can you tell me where the garden supplies are at?"

"I'm on the phone," said Howard.

John stepped closer to Howard to have his complete attention.

"Well, get off your phone and help a customer. It's your job, after all."

Howard was still listening to hold music. He took the phone away from his ear and looked at John.

"You are right, sir. I do need to take care of you first. My fault," said Howard.

Howard grabbed one of the dvds John had in his cart. Then he threw the movie in the general direction of the garden supplies section.

"The garden section is that way! Why don't you go check it out for yourself and get back to me!"

John looked back at Howard with disgust. He grabbed his cart and shuffled off to go collect his movie before somebody else swept it up.

Howard returned to his phone. He was still on hold. Howard started to walk away from the area. He had to keep moving.

Jennifer scrambled through the crowd of people. She shoved her hands over her ears to lessen the noise in her head. She did not want to deal with anybody at the moment.

"No. No. I'm not helping anybody right now. I'm busy. Excuse me. Excuse me. Get out of my way!"

Jacob Adams watched as she fought her way through the crowd. Then Jennifer exited through one of the service doors. She vanished to the back room. Jacob followed her path.

The flood of customers continued to venture into BestMart. Harry sat on a stool at the front entrance and greeted every customer that walked in.

"Howdy… howdy… howdy…" he repeated over and over again.

A phone in the podium nearby rang and rang. It would not stop and Harry simply ignored it. Answering that phone was not his job. It was the security officer's phone. Harry assumed Chuck left it when he went to make another round through the parking lot. Harry would let Chuck know somebody was calling for him when he returned.

"Howdy… howdy… howdy…"

Becky remained hidden. She was now completely enclosed in one of the dressing rooms. It still did not stop the customers from finding her. All of the doors had openings on the bottom and they could see her feet while she sat on the bench in the little area.

The sound of the customers roared through the thin walls of the dressing room. Becky ignored it as best as she could. She kept looking at her phone. There was a power outlet in the dressing room. She could be in there all day if she wanted.

"Can I please have some help?" asked a customer outside the door.

"I'm sorry, this area is out of order. I can't help you at the moment," said Becky.

Becky went back to her phone. She ordered a pair of shoes from the BestMart digital store.

"I just have one question."

"Becky rolled her eyes. She did not reply this time. It only encouraged the customers.

Instead, she began texting Jennifer.

Where are you? I'm dying here. :(

Jennifer entered the Dairy Department's cooler. The grocery side of the store was nearly empty. There were not that many sales in the food departments. Most of the customers ignored it during Black Friday. The only people that were in the area were not bothering to look for help. They were on the move. For the first time since the store opened, Jennifer was able to relax.

The cooler was cold, but it was tolerable, and

she was in a place where nobody was around. She was in peace.

Jennifer's phone started to alert her that she had a text. Jennifer ignored it for the moment. She didn't care. She just wanted to have a moment to herself. Her job was too stressful at times.

Jennifer peeked through the milk racks to look back out at the store. Customers were walking back and forth through the area. They were all trying to find the quickest path around the crowd and toward the next big sale.

Jennifer backed away from the glass doors. She did not want to be seen. Even behind several dozen gallons of milk customers could still find her if they wanted to.

The cooler door began to open. Jennifer looked around to see who was entering. Jacob Adams walked in and let the door close behind him.

"Who are you? What are you doing here?" Jennifer asked.

Jacob walked toward her.

"Get back to work," said Jennifer. "Do you see how busy we are?"

Jacob did not stop. He walked by several stacks of milk. Hanging on one pallet of milk was a long metal hook, meant for dragging crates of milk along the floor.

"I said get out of here. I will write you up," said Jennifer.

Jacob grabbed the milk hook. He let it dangle in his hand and scrape against the cold concrete floor.

"Please, just leave me alone," cried Jennifer.

Then Jacob swung the milk hook. It struck Jennifer across the face. The hook only left a scratch. Jennifer cried out for help, but the roar of the cooling fans kept her quiet. Nobody could hear her outside of the cooler.

Jacob struck her several more times. Small cuts appeared across her face and scalp.

Jennifer was on her hands and knees. She tried to crawl away from Jacob, but there was nowhere to go. He was in between her and the exit.

"Please, don't," she begged. "Don't hurt me."

Jacob stared at her through the reindeer mask. Her plea for mercy had no effect on him.

Jacob stood over Jennifer. He stepped down on her spine. Jennifer crumbled to the floor. The touch of the cold floor consumed her chest and face.

Then Jacob reached down with the milk hook. He secured it in Jennifer's lip and pulled back. Her cheeks were fishhooked. Jennifer was pinned down against Jacob's foot, still pressed on her spine, while the milk hook ripped into her face and arched back her head and neck.

Jennifer tried to beg and yell but she could not compose any words.

Finally, the cold steel blade of Jacob's

papercutter sliced across Jennifer's exposed throat. Blood gushed out onto the cooler floor. The blood mixed with the milk stains near the racks.

Jacob dropped Jennifer to the ground. Her head cracked against the solid ground. Then he left Jennifer's body cold and lifeless.

Chapter 17

Howard was still on hold with the BestMart customer service. Chuck was nowhere near his phone and nobody was bothering with the PA system.

He continued to keep an eye out for Jacob. The crowd was thicker than ever. Howard ignored all of the questions and complaints that the customers spewed towards him.

"There he is!"

Howard looked around. He saw John, the customer whose movie he had thrown, pointing in his direction. John had Lisa right next to him. He practically dragged Lisa with him as he charged toward Howard.

"Dammit," said Howard. Then he hung up his phone.

"This guys says you threw his movie across the store," Lisa said.

"I want this guy fired!" John demanded.

"Sir, I don't have the authority for that," said Lisa.

"Then why are you here?! Find me a manager!"

yelled John.

“Okay, alright. This is over,” said Howard. “I don’t even work here. Fire me now.”

“What?” asked Lisa.

“What!” cried out John. “Then kick this guy out! Call the cops.”

“Call the cops? For what? Making you look like the shit customer that you are?”

“He is leaving right now,” said Lisa. She pushed Howard away from John before he said anything else to the disgruntled customer.

“You better run, buddy,” said John. “Let the girl save the day!”

As Howard was dragged away by Lisa he turned as much as he could to yell back at John. “You know what? Call the cops! Get them all here. I’ll give you their number. 9-1-1!”

“Let’s go,” said Lisa. She pulled harder on Howard’s shirt to get him to move faster.

At the entrance of the BestMart, Harry was seeing the end of the stampede of customers. Space was beginning to thin out. He was saying hello fewer times.

As the crowd waned, Harry decided to start on his cleaning duties. He hopped off his chair and grabbed his swiffer mop. The once polished floor was dirt brown and covered in muck. Harry hated to see his floors like that.

He started to wipe down the area around him. Customers ignored Harry's work and walked over his clean sections.

It did not stop Harry. Then he reached closer to the door. Mixed in with the mud was a red gunk that Harry could not identify. Harry just shook his head at the mess the customers could make. Then he spritzed some cleaner onto the congealed blood and wiped it away with his mop.

A clean floor meant a presentable store.

Jacob Adams was in the Clothing Department. He stood quietly between racks of jeans and socks. None of the customers bothered him. His reindeer mask was festive, but the rest of his grungy uniform put off those around him. Many would complain about him later on their digital surveys. Until then they would just steer clear of Jacob.

The killer watched as Lisa continued to pull Howard across the store toward BestMart's entrance.

He followed.

Lisa shoved Howard toward the sliding glass doors. Since all of the management decided to disappear Lisa figured it was up to her to solve the current crisis.

"Get out," she said.

Howard stopped just inside the doorway. He

wasn't going to leave without finding Jacob first.

"Let me explain," said Howard.

"You don't even work here? You told me to look for somebody that didn't work here. Was that a joke?"

"No," said Howard. "I know how it looks. I snuck in through the back door. I used to work here, if that helps. Seriously, we are in danger."

"What? Then I'll call the cops. Why haven't you called the cops?"

"They won't listen to me anymore. Please do," said Howard.

Harry was nearby. He was nearly finished with his cleaning and Lisa and Howard were in the spot he had left to do.

As he listened to the two argue about trespassing and calling the cops he surveyed the area. Harry noticed Jacob staring at them from across the main entrance. The crowd of customers walked around him like he wasn't even there.

"Why didn't you tell us earlier?" Lisa asked Howard.

"I have," said Howard. "Nobody will listen to me anymore. I've been saying it for five years. Jacob Adams killed his brother, and now he's back to kill more people. Nobody believes it. I've been banned from the store. I had to sneak in and do it myself."

"Why should I believe you?" asked Lisa.

"You just have to," said Howard. "He was near

the entrance when the doors opened. He's wearing a mask. A reindeer mask."

Lisa's mind went into panic mode at those last few words. She remembered seeing that mask. She walked right past Jacob and didn't even know it.

"Just get out of here," said Lisa. "I'm going to call the cops. I'll tell them about you. I'll tell them about the guy in the mask."

"I am trying to help," said Howard. "Go ahead and call the cops. They should be alerted about Jacob, but please do not tell them about me."

Lisa nodded her head. She was starting to go into shock. Howard could have suggested anything and she would have simply nodded.

Harry put his swiffer away. He kept his eye trained on Jacob. The silent stalker never moved. Harry decided to investigate. Whoever the punk was that was wearing the mask, Harry wanted to know. He wanted to have the kid written up. That mask was the property of BestMart. Harry walked off and left Lisa and Howard behind.

"This is fucked up," said Lisa. "I don't know what the hell you are trying to pull. I am calling the cops. I'll tell them about Jacob, but it's because I'm calling them on you."

Howard shook his head. "I'm sorry."

Then he pulled out a gun that was tucked away behind him. It was his final plan against Jacob.

Howard grabbed Lisa by the arm. He held the gun close to her.

"Holy shit," said Lisa. Then she froze. She didn't want to anger Howard any further.

"I'm not leaving until I find Jacob. If you call the cops then you only call them on him, not on me. I'm trying to help."

"Please don't shoot me," said Lisa.

"Then let's walk," said Howard. "We can look together."

Jacob began to walk away from the main entrance. He walked directly into the candy aisle. It was near empty. The candy that was on sale was wiped clean.

Harry followed Jacob into the aisle. When he came into full view he saw Jacob standing at the other end. Jacob was no longer moving. He had his back to Harry and the rest of the aisle.

"Who are you?" Harry asked as he approached his suspect.

Jacob did not move.

"You should be working, not spying on some girl. None of you are trained well."

Harry continued to approach Jacob. The old man was growing aggravated.

"Don't just stand there. Get going."

Then Jacob turned around. The reindeer eyes

stared back at Harry.

"That is my mask. You stole that from the display. I'm going to speak to the managers about you."

Then Jacob walked forward. The blade reached out and cut into Harry's side. Harry stumbled back. His face became pale. Blood stained his shirt and clothes. It dripped down to the clean floors.

"Help… help…" Harry moaned. He was growing weaker. His voice was nothing but a whisper.

Jacob came face to face with Harry. Harry could see his own reflection in the mask. He could see himself dying.

Then Jacob covered the man's mouth to prevent him from crying out for help and gasping his last breath.

Chapter 18

Howard urged Lisa to walk through the crowd. He made sure to keep his gun close to her. Every now and then he would press the barrel up against her arm to remind her to stay close.

"We're just going to walk around. No big deal. We'll walk slowly. I saw him here. He's wearing a mask."

Lisa could not talk. She was too afraid. She wasn't afraid of the Jacob Adams threat. She was afraid of the gun pressed to her back.

"Just keep calm. I'm not going to hurt you," said Howard.

Suddenly, a scream raced through the crowd. All heads turned in that direction. Howard and Lisa paused to see what the commotion was.

"They have more smart TV's over here!"

With the new development the rush of customers changed direction. They knocked Howard and Lisa back. Then the two were torn apart.

Lisa was free. She did not waste the opportunity. She made a run for it.

"No!" shouted Howard. "No. Come back here."

Lisa disappeared into the crowd.

She kept her head down and she never looked back. She was too afraid Howard would find her again.

Her retreat led Lisa to the cash registers. There was an opening between two long lines and Lisa ran through it. Then she ducked down behind the counter. She was sure Howard had not seen her yet.

"Where's the phone? Is there a phone?" Lisa asked the employee at the register, Shannon.

"What? Who are you? Get out of here," said Shannon.

"Just give me a phone."

"Excuse me," said the customer waiting to be checked out. "I'm being checked out. Are you going to be checking us out now?"

"What's the number for security?" Lisa asked. She ignored the customer complaint.

Shannon simply stared at her deranged coworker.

"What's the number?!"

"405," said Shannon.

"Is there a problem here? I would like to be going," said the customer.

Lisa grabbed the phone and dialed the number. She listened to it ring on the other end.

One ring.

Two rings.

Three rings.

Lisa poked her head above the counter. She scanned the area. Then she saw Howard looking around. He looked straight at her.

Lisa ducked down, but it was too late. Howard was heading directly for her.

Lisa dropped the phone and made a run for it.

The employee break room was not far away. Lisa dashed for the door. It was in clear view of Howard, but she no longer cared. She needed to find help.

Lisa made it to the door and rushed inside. The door slammed shut behind her. Heather looked up from one of the tables. She was stunned to see Lisa.

"Whoa," said Heather. "What the hell?"

"Please help me," Lisa said. "This guy has a gun. We need security."

"What the fuck? I'll call Chuck. Where is the guy?"

"He's chasing me. He's coming this way."

Heather got on her phone. She stepped back away from the door. Lisa hid behind the farthest table. Heather joined her.

The phone ringed in Heather's ear. She wasn't bothering with Chuck's work line. She called his personal cell phone.

The door to the break room opened. Lisa tensed up. She didn't know what Howard was going to do.

The door opened. Heather heard the familiar sound of Chuck's ring tone. Then Chuck entered the break room. He was casually walking through the doorway. He looked at his phone. Then he looked up at Heather. Then he looked back at his phone.

"Are you calling me?" Chuck asked.

"Where have you been?!" Lisa shouted.

"What did I do?" Chuck asked.

"Somebody is out there with a gun. He was following Lisa," said Heather.

Chuck stood up straight. He cracked down and became much more serious.

"What did he look like? Do you know who it was?" Chuck asked. He had several more questions, but held off. He needed Lisa to stay coherent.

"No," said Lisa. "It was some guy pretending to work here. He told me he was looking for somebody named Jacob."

Chuck sighed at the last bit. He knew exactly who it was.

"Okay," said Chuck. "I will handle this. Stay here. I know him. I'll talk to him."

"Jacob?" Heather asked. "Wait, is it Howard?"

"Yes," said Chuck.

"He's still on that whole Jacob thing?" Heather enquired.

"Who know him?" Lisa asked.

"He used to be the manager here," said Heather.

"He was a good guy."

"He put a gun up to me!"

"WAS a good guy," said Heather.

The door to the break room opened again. Lisa screamed. It was Howard.

"That's him!" she shouted.

Chuck charged forward. He confronted Howard face to face.

"I don't want any trouble, Chuck," said Howard. He put his hands up. He kept his fingers away from the trigger on his gun.

"A little late for that, Howard," said Chuck. He disarmed the former manager. "You're under arrest."

"Please, just listen to me," said Howard. "Jacob is here. I've seen him. He wants to hurt people. I know it."

Chuck grabbed Howard's hands and put them behind his back. Then he secured them together with a ziptie.

"Just make sure everybody is okay. He's out there," said Howard.

"Nothing has happened," said Chuck. "Nothing is going to happen. You're breaking into the store now. You kidnapped an employee. Howard, will you look at yourself? You've lost it."

Howard looked over at Lisa. "I'm sorry."

Lisa didn't say anything. She turned away from him.

"I've got it from here. I'll take him to the office and call the police. Everything will be okay."

Then Chuck escorted Howard out of the break room and through the building.

Heather walked with Lisa back toward the entrance to the BestMart. They ignored any customers that approached them. Lisa was near tears. She was finally letting her emotions catch up to the rest of the day.

"You should go home," said Heather. They arrived at the front entrance. Harry's chair was abandoned. The customers walked in un-greeted.

"You've been through enough," said Heather. "You should probably just never come back at this rate."

Lisa stared at the empty chair nearby.

"Where is Harry?" Lisa asked.

"I don't know," said Heather. "Probably on one of his special breaks."

Lisa could not take her eyes off of the empty chair. Her thoughts raced to Howard's words.

"What about Taylor? Have you seen him lately?"

"No," said Heather. "He's probably in the bathroom hiding. I told you he is lazy. He does this every other day."

"But two people are missing," said Lisa.

"Don't let it get to you. There is always

somebody missing. They're either hiding or just somewhere else in the store. I haven't seen Clark and Jana for a while either, or Richard, or Jennifer. It's Black Friday. People do not like to work on Black Friday.

"Now, calm down. Don't let Howard get to you. Take the rest of the day off. I'll talk to Richard and Dustin when I see them later. I'll tell them what happened. You'll be fine. Go home. I have to get back to work. Nobody else is taking charge around here."

Heather gave Lisa a hug then walked back into the crowd of shoppers. She had to get back to work.

Lisa longed for the exit. She could call this day over, even at such an early morning. The sun was not out yet.

Then she looked back at Harry's empty chair.

Lisa walked back into BestMart.

Chapter 19

Chuck brought Howard to the HR's office. It was away from the customers and the employees. He could secure Howard in there until the police arrived.

"Why don't you believe me?" Howard asked as they approached the office door.

"I'm sorry, Howard," said Chuck. "Frankly, there is no reason to believe you. What happened was tragic. It was horrible and nobody should have had to witness it. But putting the blame on some kid is crazy. You need to work past this. It wasn't Jacob's fault. And it damn well sure wasn't your fault. It was an accident."

Chuck went to open the door but the lock was broken. He tried to turn the key, but the handle was smashed. Chuck pushed up against the door, but the door would not budge. They were locked out of the office.

Lisa cautiously walked into the men's restroom. She shyly stuck her head in first to see if anybody was there.

"Hello?" she called out. There was no reply.

Then she walked in.

The restroom was quiet. In the corner of the room was the cleaning supplies cart and mop. It looked like it hadn't been touched in hours.

Lisa continued to poke around the room. She opened the first stall. It was empty.

Then she opened the second. Empty as well.

It was the same for the third stall.

Then Lisa approached the final stall in the restroom. It had an Out of Order sign posted on the door.

Before Lisa could open the last bathroom stall the door to the restroom opened. A man walked in. He froze when he saw Lisa. Before she could say a word the man took several steps back, afraid he was in the wrong restroom.

"Sorry," said Lisa. "Maintenance. I'll get out of here."

Lisa put her head down and scurried out of the men's restroom. She was embarrassed to be seen in there and to think she would have found a clue to some kind of murder spree.

Heather sat on Harry's stool. The old man had not returned and Heather was getting anxious. She wanted to be elsewhere, but somebody had to watch the door. BestMart's best practices called for somebody to greet every customer, even when they were leaving.

"Thank you for coming. Thank you," said Heather to the customers over and over again. "Have a good day. Please come back soon. Remember to shop the best!"

Heather looked at her watch. She was growing exhausted. Everybody could take a break, but her.

She stretched out her body, first her legs then her arms, and finally her neck. As she moved her neck from side to side Heather looked up at the circular mirror above the entrance. She could see Jacob walking toward her.

"Damn it, Taylor," said Heather. "Is that you? What is with the mask? We are really busy. I don't have time for this shit."

Jacob came up to Heather. He put his arm around her then shoved the blade into her back.

Heather could feel it cut into her back. Pain shot through her entire body then she was numb. Heather looked at the reindeer face. It wasn't Taylor.

Her movement was gone. Blood drained from her face. The blade twisted in her back. Then she was gone.

Heather's body went limp. Jacob caught her before she stumbled to the floor. The customers around them were so focused on entering BestMart and searching for the best way to get around they never noticed Jacob or his latest victim.

Jacob propped Heather against his side and

walked her toward the benches along the wall of the entrance.

A teenage boy with massive headphones was asleep on one of the benches. His music blared beyond his ears, but the guy was unphased. Jacob placed Heather's body down beside him. He slipped off her work vest, and gently placed her head on the boy's shoulder.

Jacob Adams left the sleeping couple. He wandered back into the BestMart.

Chapter 20

Lisa foolishly returned to the main entrance of the BestMart. She was embarrassed to think she wanted to find some kind of horrific scene. It was time for Lisa to go home.

As she walked toward the exit, Lisa saw Heather slumped down on one of the benches. The sleeping teenager kept her propped up.

Lisa walked over to Heather to tell her she was right. Lisa was just being paranoid.

"Really, Heather?" Lisa joked. "Wake up. Who else is going to run this place?"

Lisa tapped Heather on the shoulder, but there was no response. The sleeping teenager next to Heather began to stir. He could barely hear Lisa through the sound of his blaring headphones.

"Wake up, Heather," said Lisa. She shook Heather harder.

Then Heather's body fell forward into the lap of the customer next to her. Her wounds and bloodstains became visible on her lower back.

The boy screamed. He flailed his arms in an

attempt to push Heather's body off of him. Then he simply charged to his feet. Heather's body crashed to the floor. She left a blood trail down the boy's jeans and onto his shoes.

"Oh my god, oh my god, oh my god," the guy repeated.

Lisa hurriedly knelt down to embrace Heather. Her brain was not registering that Heather was dead.

"Heather! Heather!" she screamed into the dead girl's ear in the hope it would wake her up. "Somebody call for help! Help!"

The crowd of customers continued to walk around the troubled BestMart employee. They were either too busy trying to get into the store or in a hurry to escape the madness.

Lisa held Heather in her arms. Only one thought became apparent: Howard was right.

Lisa jumped to her feet. Nobody was listening to her. Nobody would help. She was going to have to do it herself.

Jacob Adams stalked the crowd outside of the Toy Department. The grand display of Battlebear actions figures was down to ruins. The only toys left were several of the side characters and variations that never appeared on the show.

It did not stop the parents from diving through the now chaotic pile of toys to see if there were any good choices left.

Jacob listened as a young boy demanded from his mother one of the Red Battlebears.

"You promised me a new toy!" he whined.

"You can have a new one," said his mother. She presented her son Ace Tork. He was one of the mechanics for the Red Battlebear.

"No!"

"That's all they have left," she said.

"I don't want him!"

"Well, it's him or nothing." Then the mother grabbed her son's hand and escorted him away from the toys.

Jacob watched as they passed him and began to walk toward the exit. The little boy started to cry and scream.

Jacob started to follow them.

Chuck and Howard were stuck outside of the HR office. Chuck could not get the door to budge. Something was keeping it jammed.

Howard sat on the floor against the wall. He found the comfiest position he could with his hands secured behind his back.

Lisa ran up to them. She was out of breath, but it did not stop her.

"Heather," she said between giant breaths. "Heather has been stabbed."

"What?" Chuck said. He completely forgot about the door.

"She's dead," said Lisa. "Somebody killed her."

Chuck stared down Howard. "What did you do?"

"I didn't do anything," defended Howard. "I've been with you the whole time. We saw her alive. It's Jacob. It's Jacob. I'm so sorry."

Chuck thought for a second. He looked at Howard and Lisa. Then he looked back at the office door.

"We can't start a panic. We need to find him. There are security cameras in the office, but I can't get in."

"Just break down the door!" Howard exclaimed.

"Fine," said Chuck.

Chuck took a fire extinguisher that was hanging on the wall near the office door. He used it as a battering ram against the door handle. After several hits the door creaked open.

The lights were off. Only the white light from the black and white monitors illuminated the room. As light poured in from outside the room, Lisa, Chuck, and Howard could see several shadows scattered throughout the room.

Chuck pushed the door open as far as it would go. A dolly and a giant plastic tub blocked it from opening very wide. Chuck reached for the light switch to get a better look inside.

"Hello?" Lisa called out.

Then the lights came on.

The horrors in the room were revealed.

Dead bodies of BestMart employees sat in two different chairs and the rest were flopped on the ground. The inside of the plastic tub was covered in blood.

"Oh, my god," said Lisa. She saw Harry, Richard, Haley, Jana, and Clark.

"Get out of here. Get out of here!" ordered Chuck.

The three of them rushed out of the office. Chuck slammed the door behind him. Howard paced back and forth. His resolve was stronger than ever.

"Get me out of these," Howard demanded. "I can help. I can find Jacob."

Chuck shook his head, but he pulled out his knife and cut through the plastic ziptie that was holding Howard's hands behind his back.

"We need to get these people out of here as fast as we can," said Chuck.

The three of them ran over to the checkout stands. They found an empty register. Chuck was quick to grab the phone. He punched in the code to use the intercom. Then he handed the phone to Lisa.

"Here," he said. "They'll listen to a girl. Just be calm. You don't want to start a panic. Just announce that the store is closed."

Lisa braced the phone up to her face. She took a deep breath.

"Attention shoppers, BestMart will be closing immediately. Please leave as quickly as you can. I'm sorry for the inconvenience. Have a great day!"

The announcement went all through the store. Every customer looked up in anger and confusion. It wasn't even dawn yet. There was still plenty of time for Black Friday shopping. There was no way BestMart was closing.

The anger from the customers fed off of each other. They began demanding answers from unprepared employees. The only response was a blank stare and a shrug of the shoulders.

"What do you mean you are closing?"

"Do you know how long I was outside? I'm not going anywhere!"

"I have all this stuff. I am buying it. Take me to a register."

The crowd was in an uproar at the cash registers, but nobody was budging. They were committed to buying their merchandise.

"No, no, no," said Lisa. "They aren't listening."

"Get them to listen!" said Howard. He turned to the crowd and began to scream at them. "Get out of here! Everybody! You are all in danger!"

John and Blanch fought through the crowd to confront Lisa and Chuck about the turn of events.

"What is going on here? Why are you shutting down? We have a right to be here," said Blanch.

Chuck stepped forward to handle the situation.

"I'm sorry, but this is an emergency. We have to shut down. If you would please exit the building."

"No!" scolded Blanch. "The service here has been horrible today. I want to speak to a manager. Right now! I want an explanation for the terrible environment that you put on for your customers."

"You can't even apprehend that jackass," said John as he pointed toward Howard, who continued to scream at the customers about leaving the store.

"I want some kind of discount," Blanch demanded. "I have had a terrible shopping experience today."

Lisa had enough. She came face to face with Blanch.

"Listen, lady, I've had it with you. You need to leave. Stop your whining and get out of here. You are all in danger."

Blanch reeled back in disgust. She stuck her nose up to Lisa.

"Don't think I'll forget about you. You'll be hearing from me later. You lost a customer for life."

With those final words, John and Blanch turned their heads and they walked away.

"That's two down," said Chuck. "Get on the intercom again. We need to get these people out of here."

As Chuck was talking, Lisa zoned in on the fire alarm nearby.

"I have a better idea," she said.

Jacob continued his hunt of the mother and her young son. The boy never stopped crying. He dragged his feet as his mother made their way toward the registers.

"We have to go," said his mother.

Her son fought every step of the way. He started to grab on to displays and shelves to stop his mother's retreat. He wanted a red Battlebear and he wasn't going to leave until he got one.

Jacob started to close in on his prey.

"I don't know about this," said Chuck. "It could make things worse."

He and Lisa were by the fire alarm. Chuck would have preferred another solution, but there time was running out.

"It'll get people out of here. That's what counts."

"...Do it," said Chuck.

Jacob came up from behind the mother and her son. He made his strike quick. The blade cut directly into the woman's neck. She was too busy trying to pull her son away from a model display of a desk to notice Jacob approach her.

She crumbled to the floor in a puddle of blood.

The young boy screamed as he watched his mother die in front of him.

This time the crowd noticed. The customers around Jacob screamed in terror. They pushed forward through the crowd ahead of them to get away from Jacob Adams. People behind him stopped in their tracks, but the surging crowd behind them shoved them forward.

Then the fire alarm screeched across the building.

Panic consumed every customer in the BestMart.

Jacob looked up at the alarms going off. The customers around him began to swarm in every direction. They needed to escape from the imminent danger.

Then Jacob began to swing his blade wildly. He struck at anybody he could. Blood began to fly. People stumbled to the ground injured from Jacob's attack.

The customers that were left unharmed trampled over the injured in their attempt to escape. It was a battle to stay alive.

Alarms would not settle down at the BestMart entrance. The fire alarm was still blaring. Security alarms were going off triggered by emergency exits throughout the building. Merchandise with anti-theft devices were taken beyond the BestMart property. Nobody was bothering with the registers, but they were not going to leave without their shopping spoils.

"It's working!" said Lisa. "They're leaving."

"We have to get in there," said Howard. "We have to find Jacob."

"What if he's in this crowd?" Lisa asked.

"Stay here," said Chuck. "Keep an eye out for him. The cops will be here soon. If you see him get word to me, but don't approach him."

Chuck then looked at Howard.

"You're coming with me. We're going in there."

Howard nodded his head.

The two of them fought against the frightened current of customers and charged their way deeper into BestMart. They had to find Jacob before he hurt any more people.

Lisa stayed at the door. She urged the people to move cautiously out the exit.

"Keep going beyond the parking lot," she ordered. "There are a lot of people that need to leave."

Her words were lost on most of the customers. Many of them made it clear of the building then huddled to its side. They wanted to see what was going to happen next, whether the building was going to burn down or they were going to get to go back inside and finish their shopping.

Chapter 21

Jacob Adams was unstoppable. His blade swung from side to side. Unfortunate customers were hit left and right. If the wound was bad enough they would stumble to the ground. Then they trapped the bystanders coming up behind them. When that happened it gave Jacob a chance to strike out at more people. The panicked group of people could only scream.

Half a dozen bodies were on the ground. People tried to run over them, but most tripped. The lucky ones escaped with only a scratch from Jacob's blade.

One woman was shoved to the ground at Jacob's feet. Her friend had ditched her to make an easy escape. Jacob reached down and grabbed the woman by the hair. She screamed for help, but nobody came to her aid. Then Jacob slit her throat.

Chuck and Howard struggled to fight through the crowd. They kept their eyes peeled for any sign of Jacob. As they hurried down an aisle they started to notice retreating customers with wounds across their arms and legs. People were crying and calling out for help.

"Where is he?" Chuck called out.

"Where is the guy with the knife?" Howard asked to anybody who would listen.

"What is going on?" asked Becky. She had her head sticking out of the dressing room she was hiding in.

Howard ignored the young girl's question.

"Get out of here. There's a killer," said Chuck as he continued on through the crowd of bloody customers.

Becky shrieked then went back to her hiding place in the dressing room.

Jacob stood over the bodies of ten victims. It was becoming a natural barrier between Jacob and the rest of the crowd, but there were still the unlucky few.

One man struggled to carry with him a 3D printer. The box was cumbersome, but the man fought his way to get it and he wasn't going to give up his prize now.

The crowd carried him toward Jacob, and before he could turn to avoid the murderer the man was pushed into the pile of broken bodies.

He stumbled and dropped his 3D printer. It crashed to the ground. Before the man could cry out for his broken device Jacob stabbed the man in the face. He created slashes across the man's eyes. Then Jacob pushed down on the man's heart. Blood surged out and

Jacob added another victim.

Jacob Adams turned back to his stream of potential victims. His blade was stained red. It matched his jeans, shoes, and the floor under his feet.

Then a little girl was pushed onto the altar of dead bodies. She was crying uncontrollably for her mommy.

Jacob stared at the little girl. He walked over toward her. Once he was towering over her he raised his blade.

"Jacob!" Howard called out.

Jacob stopped. He turned around and looked up to see Howard standing on the edge of the dead.

Chuck made his move while Jacob was distracted. He rushed in and grabbed the little girl. Jacob was not quick enough to strike at Chuck before he could get clear.

Jacob swung wildly and only hit air. Then he stopped and turned back to Howard.

Chuck pushed through the crowd with the girl in his arms. He stopped on the other side of the aisle, clear from any danger.

"Are you okay?" he asked the little girl.

The little girl nodded her head. Tears were still welling in her eyes.

"Good, good," said Chuck. He brushed the hair out of her face. "I need you to do something for me. I need you to find a police man, a fireman, anybody like that. Send them here. Can you do that?"

The little girl nodded her head.

"What about my mommy?" she asked.

"You can find your mommy, too," said Chuck. "I'll even help you find her later if you can't. But right now I need help against that bad man."

The little girl nodded her head again.

"Good!" said Chuck. "You can do it. Please be careful. Don't stop until you get out of the building."

Then he pointed the girl in the right direction and set her off for help. He and Howard were going to need it.

Meanwhile, the crowd was beginning to thin out. There were only a handful of people left in the BestMart and they were staying clear of Jacob and the massacre around him.

"It's over, Jacob," said Howard. "You're done."

Jacob stared at Howard. The reindeer mask was tainted with his victim's blood. The rosy red nose was now dark blood red.

Jacob charged forward with his blade at the ready. Howard reached up to stop Jacob from bringing down his weapon. The two combatants struggled against each other's strength.

The blade waved dangerously in the air. Jacob slowly forced it down toward Howard. Howard tried to keep it away, but Jacob was stronger than he was.

Howard watched as the blade pressed up against his shoulder. It cut through his clothes and deep into his skin. He screamed out in pain. The reindeer looked at its latest work. Then it turned back to look Howard in the eye.

Howard looked into the hollow eyes of Jacob Adams' new face. Then Howard's strength began to return. He pushed Jacob off of him. The blade cut across his shoulder as Jacob pulled away, but Howard did not feel a thing. He could not let Jacob get away again.

Jacob steadied himself. Howard did not wait for Jacob to attack. He charged forward. Jacob did not have time to prepare his blade. Howard crashed into the killer. He knocked the papercutter out of Jacob's hand. It clanked against the floor.

Howard wrapped his arms around Jacob's head in an attempt to suffocate and secure Jacob. Jacob fought to get Howard off of him. Wild punches hit Howard, but the former manager would not let go.

Then Howard reached up. He pushed his thumb into Howard's fresh wound. Pain flushed through Howard's arm and upper body. He lost his grip of Jacob and screamed out in agony.

Jacob grabbed his blade, and got back to his feet. Howard turned away from Jacob to retreat. Jacob struck. He sliced across Howard's back several times.

Each time Howard screamed in pain.

Howard stumbled to the ground. Jacob had defeated him.

Then Chuck charged back into the fight. He tackled Jacob to the ground. The bodies on the floor created an uneven surface. Chuck lost his footing and his fall went wild. The two of them landed hard on the ground. Chuck rolled through the pile of bodies. Jacob fell straight on his back, but he managed to hold on to his blade.

Jacob was quick to recover. He reached back to his feet and attacked Chuck. Chuck tried to get back to his feet, but he was too slow in his position; wedged between two dead bodies.

Jacob did not waste any time. He ambushed Chuck and pierced the security guard's heart with his blade. Chuck struggled to fight away the attack but it was too late. He felt his last bit of pain and collapsed into the pile of the dead.

Jacob stood up tall. The area was clear. All that was left was Howard. Jacob's accuser writhed in pain on the ground, defenseless against the masked killer.

Chapter 22

The parking lot was filled with former BestMart customers. Nobody had left the premises. There was too much fear going through the crowd. There were injured that needed to be tended to, and there were still purchases that needed to be made.

Lisa remained at the door to guide people out of the building. Very few other BestMart employees helped her. They either didn't know what was going on, were too scared to help, or simply didn't care.

The little girl that Chuck had saved early came up to Lisa. She tugged on her vest until Lisa looked down.

"Hello," said Lisa.

"They told me to find a police officer. I don't see any," said the little girl. "You look helpful."

"Who told you?" asked Lisa.

"Some man," said the little girl. "There was a scary reindeer attacking people. The man saved me."

"Is he still in there?"

The little girl nodded her head yes.

Lisa looked back into the store. The crowd was

almost out of the building, but there was still no sign of Chuck, Howard, or even Jacob.

"Okay," said Lisa. "Keep looking for the police officers. Send them in. Tell them what you told me. I'm going to go in and help."

Then Lisa left the little girl. She ventured back into BestMart and the Black Friday Massacre.

Jacob stood tall over Howard. The killer toyed with his latest victim. He stepped on Howard's fingers and slowly crushed the man's hand. Howard yelled and cursed but could no longer fight Jacob away from him. Jacob cut his knife across Howard's back several times. He was taking his time with this kill.

Lisa heard the screams across the store. She approached the area cautiously. Jacob was standing in the middle of the pile of bodies. His back was to Lisa as she walked forward.

Howard continued to cry out in pain and anguish. Jacob was not relenting. Lisa winced every time Howard pleaded for mercy.

Lisa started to regret her decision. She looked over the pile of bodies. She saw Chuck's dead face frozen in a moment of terror.

Then the screaming stopped. Lisa looked over. Howard was not moving. Jacob stood up straight. He looked over Howard's still body.

Lisa decided to retreat. She had to keep her

distance. The cops would be there any minute.

As she stepped backward, Lisa was not paying attention to where she was going. She tripped over several discarded movies that were scattered across the floor.

She managed to catch herself before she fell, but all the noise she made alerted her presence to Jacob Adams. Jacob turned around and stared directly at Lisa.

"No, no, no," said Lisa. "Go away."

Jacob began his march in her direction.

Lisa made a run for it.

She raced through the obstacle course of discarded items and shopping carts left over by customers. Lisa looked back every few seconds. Jacob was still following her.

Lisa did not head for the exit. She was afraid what would happen if Jacob got close to more innocent people. The store was empty. She could keep him busy while the cops arrived.

She ran down the aisle and came to the Hunting and Recreation Department. Behind the counter were dozens of guns and bullets of all sizes.

Lisa jumped the counter and tried to pry open the door that blocked her from an offensive weapon. The glass door would not budge.

Jacob was getting closer.

Lisa did not have time. She reached over and

grabbed whatever she could. Boxes of shells were behind the counter. She started to throw them at Jacob. They simply bounced off the unrelenting pursuer.

Jacob entered the Hunting Department.

Then Lisa slammed down on the glass case in front of her. Shards of glass exploded into the air. They caught Lisa across the arm, but it did not stop her.

She reached down and got hold of one of the hunting knives that was on display in the glass counter.

Jacob stopped and stared at Lisa across the counter.

"Stay away from me!" she yelled. She pointed the seven-inch knife at Jacob.

Her threat did not last long. Jacob continued his chase. He walked forward toward Lisa with his own longer blade ready to strike.

Lisa charged forward. She jumped over the counter to confront Jacob head on. Lisa drove the knife into Jacob's chest. Then she pulled it out and struck him several more times.

Jacob stopped in his tracks. He dropped his blade. Then he fell to the ground in front of Lisa.

Lisa stumbled backward. The bloody knife trembled in her hand. Jacob was sprawled on his back a few feet away.

It was over. Lisa could hardly believe it. The wounds on her arm started to creep into her mind. It began as a pinch, but slowly become more painful. Blood dripped down her arm. Her ankle was twisted.

Then Jacob sat up.

His breathing was louder than ever. It amplified across the empty store. Lisa stared at her stalker. He was returning to his feet.

Her strength was gone. She was spent. She thought it was over. Her legs were like jelly. She forced herself to her feet, but she didn't know how long she could last.

Jacob charged forward. He knocked the knife out of Lisa's hand. It skidded across the floor out of Lisa's reach.

Lisa turned to run away. Her legs were gaining traction. Fear brought them back to life.

Jacob reached out and stabbed Lisa across the arm. The blow was enough to knock Lisa off balance. It slowed her down, and Jacob was able to catch up to her.

He raised his blade for the final blow.

Then Howard rushed forward. He knocked Jacob back.

Blood dripped down his back. He protected his right hand while he moved. Lisa was relieved to see him.

"Come on!" he said. He offered his left arm to Lisa to help her to her feet.

Quickly, Lisa was up and moving again. She and Howard made a run for it. They wanted to get as far away as they could from Jacob Adams.

Jacob watched his retreating victims. Then he went in pursuit.

Chapter 23

Lisa and Howard stumbled through the aisles. Both were too weak to go at a full run. They braced against each other to keep from falling over.

Lisa kept looking back to see if they were being followed. The coast was clear. They had to get out. There was nothing left they could do.

Then Jacob Adams walked out of an aisle in front of them. He stood, menacingly, in their path.

"Nooo!" screamed Lisa.

Jacob began to walk toward them.

"This way," said Howard. He pointed for Lisa to turn into the aisle on their left. Howard was losing his strength. Lisa had to practically carry Howard with her. They stumble together toward the end of the aisle and the next opening. It led toward the edge of the store.

"There," said Howard. His voice was growing weaker. He gestured toward a doorway twenty feet away. It was the entrance to the Home and Garden Department.

Jacob kept up the chase. He was never out of sight of Lisa and Howard since he reemerged in front of them.

Lisa and Howard entered the Home and Garden Section. As soon as they passed the doorway Howard collapsed out of Lisa's arms.

"No!" said Lisa. She bent down and grabbed Howard to pull him back up, but Howard waved her off.

"Get out of here," said Howard. "You need to hide. Get in a trashcan. Get behind shit. Just get out of here."

"You're coming with me," said Lisa.

They could see Jacob approaching. He was at the entrance to the department.

Howard grabbed a shovel from the nearby shelf. He was too weak to stand up, but he would be damned if he didn't defend himself.

"Go," Howard told Lisa.

Lisa looked over at Jacob. Then she looked at Howard.

Then she ran.

Jacob approached Howard. Howard swung his shovel wildly. He kept the motion going to keep Jacob at a distance.

Jacob held back. He watched the shovel circle around his target. Then he stepped forward. Jacob took the blow from the shovel. He stumbled, but was able to catch the shovel and rip it out of Howard's hands.

Defenseless, Howard put up his hands to stall any attack from Jacob. The killer kicked Howard in the gut. Then he shoved Howard down to the floor on his back.

"Get away from him!" Lisa screamed as she hit Jacob across the back with the discarded shovel.

Jacob was sent crashing into the shelving from the blow. It gave Howard another moment of reprieve.

Lisa was ready for another swing. She hit Jacob across the back for the second time. This time the shovel broke in the middle of its wooden handle. Splinters scattered across the room.

Lisa stepped back. Even with the shovel destroyed she kept it at the ready. She repositioned herself to stand between Howard and Jacob.

Jacob recovered from Lisa's attack. The killer reindeer approached.

Lisa swung her splintered stick back and forth. Jacob caught Lisa in her backswing. He knocked the weapon out of her hands. Lisa was caught off balance. Jacob stabbed her in the thigh.

Lisa's leg could no longer hold her weight. She fell to the floor. A shelf of trash bags and lawn rakes stopped her fall.

Now, Jacob stood over his two victims. Both Lisa and Howard had trouble moving. Jacob turned his head to both of them. He stared at Howard then he stared at Lisa. He went back and forth between the two of them. One of them was going to die first.

Jacob turned to Howard. He walked toward the

fallen BestMart manager. Jacob stood on Howard's knees. Howard screamed out in pain.

The reindeer face smiled down at Howard.

Then Lisa came up from behind.

She swarmed Jacob with an industrial sized trash bag. She collided with the killer and knocked the blade out of his hand.

The trash bag consumed Jacob from his head to his knees. Lisa wrapped her arms around Jacob's neck. Then she hung on for dear life.

Jacob struggled to break free from his constraints. He could not move his arms freely enough out of the bag, and he could not see. Or breathe.

He stumbled around the department. Lisa dangled from his neck. She hung freely around Jacob. Her entire grip was wrapped around his masked face.

Jacob dropped to one knee. His arms started to break free. He picked at Lisa, but she would not let go.

She could hear him desperately breathing through the dark plastic bag.

Jacob dropped closer to the ground. His hands now braced him up instead of attacking Lisa. Lisa remained on his back. Her full weight was on top of him.

Then Jacob collapsed to the ground. He went quiet. He went still.

Lisa waited. She stayed quiet. She didn't even breathe. Silence filled the department.

"He's dead," Lisa finally said.

She rolled off of the lifeless Jacob Adams. Howard watched in stunned silence. Lisa and Howard looked at each other's bloody messes.

"You did it," said Howard. "I'm so sorry."

They both did a double take on Jacob's body. It remained still.

Lisa and Howard struggled to their feet.

Howard came up to Jacob's body. He peeled away the trash bag to see Jacob in full view. Then he pulled off the reindeer mask to see Jacob's face.

Howard was met with the same blank stare he saw five years ago. There was no more emotion in him now as there was then.

He let go of the mask and it snapped back into place over Jacob's face. That was Jacob's true identity.

Then Lisa and Howard started on their final exit out of BestMart.

Chapter 24

Dawn broke over the BestMart. Customers, policemen, firefighters, paramedics all filled the parking lot. The injured were tended to while the store was barricaded off.

Lisa and Howard stumbled out of the BestMart. Officers and paramedics immediately surrounded them.

"There she is!" screamed the little girl. She pointed at Lisa for the cops to help her.

"He's in there," said Lisa. "Home and Garden."

"Who's in there?" asked one of the cops.

"Jacob Adams," answered Howard.

"He's dead," said Lisa.

Then they were escorted away from the BestMart and toward an ambulance to be checked on.

Cops swarmed the building. They walked the entire store. Every department was empty.

Including Home and Garden. All they found was a black plastic trash bag.

The customers remained outside in the BestMart parking lot. Most of them had merchandise in their hands. They were ready to get on with their lives and fill in the horrors of their day with their shiny new toys.

They lived for another Black Friday.

For updates on future projects by
Dane G. Kroll
please visit:

danegkroll.com
facebook.com/danegkroll
@DaneGKroll on Twitter

Dane G. Kroll is the writer of the kaiju series *Realm of Goryo* and fantasy series *Eluan Falls,* along with more titles in horror and children's literature.

Made in the USA
Charleston, SC
24 May 2016